Rick took her face in his hands. "I only care about keeping you safe."

His soft words turned Ginny inside out. His intense drive to protect her was one of the things she'd loved most about him, because all her life she'd been the one doing the protecting.

It had felt good to lean on someone else.

Then he'd left, and the dove hanging from her rearview mirror became her reminder that she needed to lean on God alone. Except, Rick had come back and wanted to be her protector.

Unspoken regrets shadowed his eyes. "I honestly don't know whether some psychotic protestor or one of your uncle's enemies or one of mine has targeted you. But I promise you I'll figure it out and put a stop to him."

"*I?* Uh-uh. Whether you like it or not, we're in this together. No more secrets."

He hesitated, then with assurance in his eyes, said, "I like the sound of that."

SANDRA ORCHARD

lives in rural Ontario with her real-life hero husband, two of their three children and a menagerie of pets. An arts and science graduate with a major in math, Sandra never gave up her childhood dream of becoming a writer. Yet, for many years, needlecrafts, painting and renovating their century-old home satisfied her creative appetite. Then she discovered the world of inspirational fiction.

After shelf upon shelf filled with books, her husband challenged her to write her own. And so the journey began.

For several years, she wrote while homeschooling their children. Then on her graduation day (her youngest daughter's first day of college), Sandra received the call that one of her novels had sold, and the publisher wanted more. What a blessed launch to this new phase of her life.

Sandra loves to hear from readers and can be reached through her website, www.SandraOrchard.com, or c/o Love Inspired Books, 233 Broadway, Suite 1001, New York, NY 10279.

Recycling programs for this product may not exist in your area.

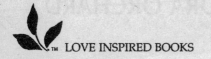

LOVE INSPIRED BOOKS

ISBN-13: 978-0-373-67480-0

DEEP COVER

Copyright © 2011 by Sandra van den Bogerd

www.LoveInspiredBooks.com

Printed in U.S.A.

DEEP
COVER

SANDRA ORCHARD

Love Inspired

There is nothing concealed that will not be
disclosed, or hidden that will not be made known.
—*Luke* 12:2

In loving memory of my mom and dad.
Forever in my heart.

THANKS TO:

My husband, Michael, for believing in my dream. My children, Christine, Paul and Jennifer, for quietly taking up the slack around the house when my writing overtakes my days, for cheering me on, praying for me, listening, critiquing and even typing!

My agent, Joyce Hart, and editor, Tina James, for believing in me. My mentors Margaret Daley and Susan May Warren for teaching me so much, and for enthusiastic encouragement.

My critiquers, Wenda Dottridge and Vicki Talley McCollum, for their selfless investment of time, and invaluable suggestions. My writing buddies, Laurie Benner and Kate Weichelt, for inspiring brainstorming sessions and chocolate celebrations!

My first readers, Betti Mace and Tina Tarling, for their timely feedback. My friend Nancy Miller for her endless support in too many ways to name. My prayer warriors, Angie Breidenbach, Lisa Jamieson and Patti Jo Moore.

The numerous police officers who shared their expertise with me.

And most important, thanks to my Lord Jesus for the greatest love of all.

ONE

Stop now, or else.

Rick Gray strode toward the spray-painted warning inside the half-framed building. The sawdust-strewn floor groaned under his weight, then suddenly gave way, dropping him ten feet onto his back in basement mud. His hard hat cracked against a rock and the air rushed from his lungs. Pain streaked through his body. He tried to suck in a breath, but his chest seized.

He willed his muscles to relax and tried again. This time a gasp squeaked through.

He squinted past the flashes of color dancing in front of his eyes and focused on the floor joists that dangled over his head. He might be an undercover cop just posing as the foreman on this group-home project, but he didn't have to be the real thing to spot the clean saw lines bisecting three of the struts.

Fury blazed through his veins. If the basement slab had been poured yesterday as planned, he'd be a dead man.

Holding his breath against the throbbing pain, Rick

crawled up the ladder to the main floor. Last night's rain had turned the Southern Ontario sandy loam into a soupy mess, and the late winter chill layering the air around Miller's Bay bit through his damp jeans. Bit like the suspicion nipping at his thoughts that this wasn't the handiwork of another disgruntled neighbor.

The warning to stop construction on the controversial home for the mentally challenged might be from an angry Not-In-My-Backyarder, but if his "boss" had figured out why Rick really took this job, staging an accident that looked like the work of local protesters was an inspired way to take him out.

Two shiny leather shoes, enveloped in thin rubber sole guards, met his nose at the top of the ladder. Rick shot out his hand and dug his fingers into the floorboards, bracing himself for the push that would send the ladder, and him, toppling back to the ground.

Emile Laud's well-manicured hand reached for Rick's free arm and hoisted him up the last three rungs. In a three-piece suit and Burberry overcoat, his boss clearly hadn't planned on picking his way across a construction site. "What happened?"

"Sabotage," Rick grunted, his suspicion of Laud masked by his struggle to pull in a full breath.

The panic that flashed in Laud's eyes wasn't the response of a man who'd just tried to kill off his foreman. His gaze traveled across the splintered wood, up Rick's mud-caked pants and paused on the cracked hard hat clutched in Rick's fist. "Are you okay?"

"I'll live." Rick watched Laud's reaction, but nothing in his expression suggested he hoped otherwise. So who was their saboteur? And what did he really want?

Laud pried a handkerchief out of his coat pocket and wiped the mud from his hands. "Those crazy radicals have gone too far this time. I've got my new PR girl stopping by this morning. We'll have her take pictures and write a news article to rally public opinion to our side."

Rick kneaded the muscles in the back of his neck. Here to nail Laud for the arson murder of two—maybe more—people, Rick couldn't afford to have an innocent get in his way. And that's exactly what would happen if this new PR person acted on Laud's suggestion. She'd become the face and voice of this project, and far too enticing a target for their saboteur.

A beat-up green Impala crested the hill beyond the site.

"Here she comes now," Laud said, motioning toward the car.

Rick's heart slammed into his aching ribs. He'd know that car—and its driver—anywhere. Ginny Bryson. The one person who could blow his cover wide open.

She may not know what he really was, but she knew he was no construction foreman. Rick braced his hand on the nearest stud and razored a breath into his lungs. His ex-girlfriend couldn't have picked a worse time to career back into his life. How was he supposed to keep her safe this time?

She parked next to Laud's BMW, and the instant her sleek legs dropped into view below the driver's door, Rick's mouth went dry. The sight of her roused memories he'd been trying to forget for fifteen long months.

The wind tousled her hair and reflexively his fingers curled. He could almost feel the silky caress of her blond tresses. In those moments when he let her take over his thoughts, he could still breathe in her lavender scent and hear the sweet ring of her laughter.

Laud tiptoed through the mud to greet his niece, and then led her across strips of plywood toward the building.

Instinctively, Rick limped into the shadows; the second Ginny looked past his new mustache and bristly hair and recognized him, she'd rat him out to her Uncle Emile. The uncle she'd claimed to *never* see.

Rick glanced skyward and prayed for a miracle.

A lone backhoe loomed on the horizon, silhouetted against the steel-gray sky, its tires caked in mud. Too bad the machine wasn't big enough to dig him out of this mess.

The last thing he wanted to do was lie to Ginny. Again.

He'd relived her betrayed expression too many times during the lonely months since the last time. Rick slapped on his hard hat and steeled himself against his regrets. He'd been undercover on another case when they met and he'd made the choice not to tell her he was a cop. There was no going back now.

Laud's hand slid like a snake across Ginny's shoulders, and Rick wanted to hurtle across the boards, rip her away from his grasp, sink his fist into Laud's pretty face and scream the truth—the man killed people. People like Tom, and that old woman, trapped in her wheelchair as smoke ate the breath from her lungs.

Instead, Rick shoved his fists into his coat pockets and hobbled toward them, trying to conceal the pain still crushing his ribs. If only his partner hadn't run back into the burning building, he'd still be alive.

Rick shook the image from his mind. Given the trail of dummy companies and insurance claims he'd unearthed following Tom's death, Rick had no doubt that Laud torched his real estate for the insurance money, but Ginny would never believe his story. Her uncle had done too good a job covering his tracks by playing the town philanthropist. And in Ginny's eyes, Rick was nothing more than something she'd scrape off her shoes.

He'd let her keep that misconception, too, because once again, he had a job to finish. A job she could jeopardize if she knew what he really was—an undercover cop who wanted to dump her uncle in the dankest, darkest, dirtiest prison cell the province had to offer.

Ginny turned and, for an instant, Rick forgot his mission as he drank in the flush of her cheek. The sparkle in her eyes. The ever-present smile.

He took a second to enjoy the fact she still looked wonderful, uncontaminated by the scum he crossed paths with on a regular basis. The scum he'd wanted to protect her from. Yes, he'd made the right choice when he let her walk away believing he was a lying lowlife.

He'd been fooling himself to think he could shield her from the danger of his profession. While out at dinner with Ginny, he hadn't been wearing the acid-washed jeans and tattooed jacket that flagged him as a fellow gang member, but that hadn't stopped Snake from recognizing him. And if the thought of what Snake might do to her if he'd figured out Rick was a cop hadn't convinced him to let Ginny walk away, her horrified who-are-you expression would have.

Ginny blinked once and then again more deliberately.

He'd forgotten how strikingly green her eyes were, like a forest he could get lost in for hours. Only now they seemed to be measuring him and finding him wanting. Her smile wilted, and just once he wished he could see trust in those eyes again. Laud's next words obliterated that hope.

"Duke, this is my niece, Ginny Bryson. Ginny, meet my foreman, Duke Black."

Ginny's gaze snapped to her uncle, then locked on Rick. "Duke?" she said, and then clearly struggling over how to respond, repeated stupidly, "Duke?"

The memory of her parting words—*you lied to me*—knifed through his thoughts. All these months later, nothing had changed.

Rick thrust out his hand and put as much enthusiasm into his voice as he could muster with the black clouds looming overhead. "Good morning, Miss Bryson. I look forward to working with you." He held his breath, praying she would play the game.

Her hand met his easily. Too easily.

He'd forgotten how delicate her fingers felt, how soft against his work-worn palm.

"I used to know a guy..." she said slowly, as though savoring each word. "He looked a lot like... you."

"Really?" He struggled to sound unfazed even as the specter of a saboteur targeting Ginny strangled his breath. "I get that a lot."

Ginny pulled her hand back and folded her arms over her chest. "Yeah, his name was Rick."

Shivers of frustration and anger played havoc with Ginny's insides as Rick, or Duke, or whatever he called himself these days, darted a glance at Uncle Emile. This project was too important to her to put at risk. Why should she care if Rick got into trouble?

She should've blurted the truth about his alias on the spot, not let his pleading eyes win her sympathy. How dare he put her in this position? It was Uncle Emile—deceived by Rick's lies—that she should be worried for. When she dropped *Duke's* real name, her uncle had been too distracted by the sudden arrival of his secretary to hear. But the beads of moisture on Rick's forehead didn't look like raindrops.

Good. Maybe he'd do the smart thing and quit before she really blew the whistle on him.

Uncle Emile's secretary handed him a file folder through her car window, said a few words and then drove off.

Tucking the folder under his arm, Uncle Emile returned to Ginny's side. "I have to go. Duke, I'll leave you to discuss that other matter with my niece."

A light that said "with pleasure" glimmered in Rick's eyes.

Ginny grabbed her uncle's arm. "There is no way I'm working with him."

Her uncle gave Rick-slash-Duke a once-over, while Rick had the gall to just stand there—the picture of innocence. "He looks a little rough, but you'll like him once you get to know him."

Rough? Her uncle should've seen Rick with his head shaved. This new soldierlike buzz cut made him look almost decent.

But she knew better than to trust appearances. She'd give him one more chance to bow out, and if he was too cocky to take it, he'd be sorry.

Uncle Emile paused at the door of his BMW. "It's not as if the two of you will work together that closely. But for today, Duke's your man. He'll answer all your questions."

Oh, she doubted that.

As soon as Uncle Emile drove away, she turned on Rick. "What are you doing here?"

His steel-blue eyes searched hers, slowly, thoroughly. "It's good to see you again, Ginny."

Her name toppled from his lips with a huskiness that made her skin tingle. Long-buried feelings resurfaced, more fervent than ever. She dug her fingernails into her palms and fought to escape the emotional ambush.

In the distance, thunder rumbled, low and ominous.

"Do you seriously think I'll fall for your smooth talk a second time?" Her mind reeled back to the day they'd met. From the moment she'd seen him across the gym, those magnetic eyes had compelled her to look past the intimidating bald-guy appearance to the man inside. And his patient coaching of the special-needs kids had won her heart.

His gaze dropped to the ground. "I never meant to hurt you."

Right. Like after dating for two months, his easy camaraderie with the leering gang member who'd spotted them outside a restaurant in Hamilton shouldn't have upset her. She could still remember how the creep's tongue made a slow circuit around his lips and then flicked out of his mouth like the tongue of the snake tattooed on his arm. And Rick's "Hey, bro!" followed by his nervous glance at her. And the near-total transformation from the security guard he'd claimed to be into the gang member he clearly was.

Oh yeah, he'd been into security all right—how to bypass it. She hadn't needed to hang around and listen to the rest of Snake Man's loosely veiled robbery scheme to figure that out. Or to figure out that Rick wasn't the God-fearing man he'd let her believe.

She'd ended the relationship on the spot. Almost changed her phone number, even contemplated moving, but she hadn't needed to bother. He didn't attempt to defend himself, let alone try to see her again.

"How's Lori doing? Still playing basketball?" he asked now, and the warmth in his tone stole Ginny's thunder.

He'd always been kind to her mentally challenged sister. Part of her longed to know *that* Rick again. But she'd never *really* known him, had she?

"Stop answering my questions with questions. I don't know why you lied to my uncle about who you are, but I expect you to resign immediately." She'd promised she'd see this group home finished and she wasn't about to let Lori, or their dying mother, down by inviting trouble.

Rick's gaze darted to the newest spray-painted threat. "Since when do you fundraise for building projects? You told me you wrote web copy."

The irritation in Rick's voice scraped away any vestige of hope that the man Ginny once loved had been real. "How dare you make *me* sound like the one pretending to be someone I'm not? If you don't quit, I *will* tell my uncle you're an imposter."

"It's not what you think."

"Oh? And what am I thinking, Rick? Is Rick even your real name? I have no idea who you are. How can you know what I'm thinking?"

Rick glanced down at the hard hat he twisted in his hands. "All I'm asking is for a chance to start over. I really need this job."

"Yeah, a guy who switches identities every year would. And lying about who you are—that's a great way to start over." She straightened her shoulders. "I don't know who you expected to see out here today, but from the shocked look on your face, I'm certain it wasn't me. So don't feed me any more lines about starting over. I need a man who knows right from wrong. A man without any shadows in his life. A man like my uncle Emile. Someone honorable."

If not for the flinch in Rick's cheek, his face might've been carved from stone—kind of like his heart. Except not even the gray drizzle that streamed unchecked down those angular planes could douse the fire in his eyes.

"Now, if you don't mind, I'd like to see how this project is coming along."

Rick blocked her path like a giant Beware sign in his yellow rain slicker, arms akimbo. "It's too dangerous for you to wander around out here."

Ginny pushed past him, but at the sight of the sheared floor joists spearing into the basement her retort lodged in her throat. "What happened?"

"Someone cut through the timbers."

"I can see that. But why?"

"I don't know. And until I do, I don't want you around here or getting your name and picture in the papers. You could get hurt."

"Are you nuts? We need to call the police."

"You don't want to do that."

"Why?" She tore her gaze from the splintered floor and glared at him. "Are you afraid the police will pin this on you?"

"Will you forget about our past for one minute and listen? If you bring the police out here, sirens blaring, the press will be on this faster than vultures on roadkill. Is that the kind of publicity you want?"

Her chest deflated. No, definitely not. "Who would do this?"

"It could be anyone. Emile thinks it's the protesters, but a businessman like your uncle has undoubtedly amassed a number of enemies."

"That's ridiculous."

"We have to consider all the possibilities."

"We?" Ginny planted her hands on her hips. "You're quitting, remember? I will look into this myself."

Rick reached out, but then let his hand drop just shy of grazing her cheek and took a step back. "I hurt you, and for that I am sorrier than you could possibly know. But falling through those boards this morning could have killed me. These people don't care who they hurt."

She gasped, noticing for the first time the crack in his helmet, the mud smeared on his jacket.

"I couldn't bear it if something like that happened to you. Let me talk with the police quietly and help them figure out who did this."

The tenderness of his offer stirred more feelings than she wanted to remember. But for all she knew this booby trap had been set by one of his gang buddies. Even if this alias thing was entirely innocent, he'd still lied. She fisted her trembling hands. "I don't know what kind of game you're playing, but you can take yourself off my project or I can have you fired. You decide."

TWO

I'm not going anywhere. Rick rammed his fist into the punching bag slung from the rafters of his garage. Outside, rain hammered the metal roof. The lone window offered nothing but a meager shaft of light to see by. Kind of like how he felt about this job.

Rick dropped his head against the punching bag and let the memories resurface—his partner's wife and daughter huddled outside the burning building, their soot-blackened clothes plastered to their bodies by the relentless rain, their eyes fixed on the door, waiting, praying Tom would stumble out with the adopted grandma he'd run back in to save. Rick pictured the tear-streaked face of Tom's little girl as she reached for her daddy's casket; he slammed the punching bag again. He couldn't bow out. Not now, not ever. Not when guys like Laud didn't care who they sacrificed.

The side door burst open.

Rick whirled around, fists raised.

"Whoa." Fellow cop Zach Davis held up his hands. "What's got you riled?"

"Nothing." Rick snatched his towel from the work-bench and dried his face.

Rain dripped from Zach's ball cap onto an already drenched T-shirt. He lifted the cap off his head and swatted it against his jeans. "Try again."

Rick balled the towel and tossed it at Zach's head.

Laughing, Zach snagged the towel with one hand and caught Rick's wrist in the other, exposing his swollen knuckles. "Woman troubles?"

Rick shoved off his hold. They'd worked together on and off for too many years to hide the truth. He pulled a couple of root beers from the minifridge and handed one to Zach. "I saw Ginny today."

"*The* Ginny?"

"Yeah." Condensation pooled on the can and dripped through Rick's fingers. "*The* Ginny."

"Let me guess. She met Duke."

Hearing his buddy say it aloud added another hundred pounds to the weight already crushing him. If he nailed Laud before the group home was finished, the publicity storm would squelch the project. Ginny would be devastated, possibly implicated.

"Why don't you come clean? It's not like the case you're on *now* puts her life in danger."

"You of all people should know why," Rick snapped, and immediately regretted it. He had enough to worry about without going back to that dark place. Zach alone knew the emotional hits he'd taken, but that didn't mean Rick wanted to talk about them. Ever.

"You can't live the rest of your life as if you have

a bull's-eye painted on your back, afraid anyone who gets too close will get caught in the spray."

"It's more complicated than that," Rick growled.

"What's complicated? You obviously still love the woman. Tell her the truth."

Rick pulled the tab on his can and took a long drink. The icy liquid pricked at his throat, like the vague sense of foreboding that pricked at his conscience. "Laud's her uncle."

The way Zach's jaw slackened would've been funny if Rick hadn't felt so miserable. Just being around Ginny for a few minutes, and as angry as she'd been with him, had stirred up all his longings. And regrets.

"When did you find out?"

"I knew all along."

"Have you lost your mind? Does Drake know? I can't believe the captain let you go in on this one. You had to know you'd run into her."

"This conversation is between you and me. Got it? When Ginny and I dated, she claimed she rarely saw her uncle. Her connection shouldn't have been an issue."

"What is Ginny's connection, exactly?"

"She's the new PR person. In charge of fundraising."

Zach pushed his fingers through his hair, then slapped on his ball cap. "Oh, man, you're cooked. Pull out before the entire operation—and your cover—go up in flames."

"I can't. I'm here to put Laud out of business. A

few days ago, I overheard a guy put the squeeze on him for fifty grand. The accent sounded Russian. If Laud owes the Russian mob that kind of cash, it's only a matter of time before he torches another property."

"You don't know that."

"Yes, I do. Someone sabotaged the construction site last night. Laud has to be getting desperate. His last project soared into six-digit overruns. He can't keep starting new projects to finance unfinished ones. He intends to use this one to cash in. I can feel it. It's the perfect setup. Skim money from the grants and donations to keep his creditors off his back. Then torch the place for the insurance before anyone catches on."

"Perfect, except for one thing."

"Yeah." Rick's breath seeped from his chest. "Ginny."

"She's bound to tell Laud you're using an alias."

"I'm counting on it," he said, not thrilled with the plan but liking it better than the alternative. "I'll admit I've had some run-ins with the law. That nugget should convince Laud I'm corruptible enough to hire to torch one of his buildings. Then I'll have him." Rick shook the tension from his shoulders. Yeah, this could work.

"What if you're wrong? What if Ginny *is* part of the *family* business?"

"She's not." Rick crushed the soda can in his hand. That kind of innuendo was precisely why he wouldn't let this assignment fall to someone else. He had to protect Ginny. He owed her that much.

Rick rubbed his still-sore ribs. He'd do whatever it took to convince her he was her best hope of getting this project built. With a saboteur on the prowl, more than her reputation was at risk.

"Consider this, my friend. If you nail her uncle, who do you think she'll blame?"

"Me. I know." Rick had no illusions about that. "Just like I know that when this case is over, we're over."

Laud switched off his bedroom lights, pressed his back to the wall and nudged aside the curtain. He hated coincidences—like the silver Ford Escort that started tailing him within hours of his visit to the insurance company.

Bad enough the insurance buffoons wouldn't pay up on the townhouse fire. Further investigation, they claimed. Sure. Now this.

He let the curtain slip into place.

He swiped the back of his hand across his moist brow and stared at the overnight bag he'd dumped on his bed. What if his pal in the Ford didn't work for the insurance company? What if he belonged to Petroski?

The slimeball probably had spies everywhere to make sure clients didn't skip town before their next loan payments. The calling card at the construction site had no doubt been his friendly reminder.

Laud stalked down the hall. The cold laminate

floor bit into his bare feet. He never should've come back to this stink-hole town where everyone knew his business before he did. He couldn't even hire a decent salesman here.

Laud snapped on his desk lamp and glanced at the glossy sales brochure for his new high-end offices. The salesman had attached a business card with his photo—slicked-back hair, gapped teeth, cheap suit. No wonder the idiot had scarcely leased half the units at the Harbor Creek development.

The muscles in Laud's neck bunched. He dug his fingers into the knots and kneaded them loose. He'd have to find another way to raise enough cash to keep Petroski off his back until Ginny came through for him.

Laud poured himself a double Scotch, tossed it back in one swallow, and waited for its magic to take effect. But the slow burn was no match for the flames smoldering in his chest.

He sank into his leather chair and tapped in the password for his online banking account. As the *please wait* circle swirled on his computer screen, Laud fed Duke's resignation letter to the shredder. The man might be just the distraction he needed to preoccupy his niece, and her meddling mother, until his plans fell into place. He should've silenced his sister-in-law when he had the chance.

His banking info blipped onto the computer screen. A lousy three grand in the account—not enough to cover a week's interest on the three million he owed Petroski, let alone a month's.

The heat in his chest intensified.

He rubbed his knuckles over his ribs and popped another antacid.

Lori smiled at him from the hand-drawn picture on the corner of his desk. The sloppy scrawl looked like a three-year-old colored it, all big heads and stick arms outlined in worn-down crayons.

His insides twisted.

The latest blackmail note lay unopened on his desk.

Popping a second antacid into his mouth, he tore open the envelope. Boldfaced letters, cut and pasted from a newspaper, read: "You'll pay. One way or another, you'll pay."

Blinding pain clawed at his chest. He clutched his shirt with one hand and grappled for the phone with the other. Punched nine—*breathe*—one—*breathe*— The pain released a fraction, then a fraction more. *Not a heart attack. Anxiety. Just anxiety.*

Laud slumped over the desk and drew in a big breath. He tried to hang up the phone. Missed. Shifted the receiver until it fit into the cradle. If he landed in the hospital, everything would collapse. He couldn't afford to give in to weakness.

He straightened, retrieved the blackmail letter and flattened out the crinkles with his palm. No instructions. No explanations. No demands.

Just threats.

But from who?

Laud flicked his lighter at the edge of the paper and let the flames eat the words.

Just words.

The phone rang.

Laud dropped the burning page into the metal waste bin and smoothed his hair.

The phone rang a second time.

He poured himself another drink, checked his appearance in the wall mirror, straightened his shirt.

On the third ring, he picked up. "Yeah."

"I finished the background check on Duke Black and you won't like what I found."

So much for my ultimatum. Ginny scraped the supper leftovers into the bin under the kitchen sink, wishing she could expunge Rick from her thoughts as easily. She had enough crises in her life with trying to stop some crazy person from disrupting the group home's progress. If she had to deal with Rick as well, *she* might be the one who needed an institution.

She'd given him two days to quit on his own. Not because she believed his woebegone story, but because the Bible says to forgive the person who sins against you. Seventy-seven times, if necessary. And the Lord knew she had plenty of experience putting that advice into practice living with an alcoholic mother.

Yet, not only hadn't Rick cooperated, he'd dismissed the security guard she had hired to patrol the grounds and had practically throttled her after she invited the press to the construction site for a photo op. If her uncle had been in town, she would've outed Rick, then and there. Tonight, she would.

Ginny glanced out the window to see if she'd need an umbrella and noticed the same gray car that had crept past the house half an hour ago.

The phone rang. Lori dashed into the kitchen, sliding to a halt as Ginny grabbed the receiver. The muffled sound of Lori's favorite game show drifted in from the living room.

"I'm calling on behalf of Mr. Laud," Uncle Emile's newest secretary said in the overly formal tone of someone trying too hard to sound professional. "He asked me to inform you that Mr. Black will attend the council meeting in his place tonight."

"What? No." The building inspector had insisted they obtain a variance after someone—their saboteur, no doubt—complained that the location of the wheelchair ramp violated the town's building codes. Facing town council would be stressful enough without adding Rick to the equation.

"Mr. Black apparently has experience dealing with government," the woman assured her and clicked off before Ginny had a chance to respond.

Yeah, the justice department. Ginny slapped down the phone. "How could he?"

Glass shattered on the floor behind her. "How could he?" Lori parroted.

Ginny spun around to scold her sister, but at the sight of Lori staring wide-eyed at the broken shards, a laugh with an hysterical edge popped out instead. Brown moppy hair framed pudgy cheeks and a broad, flattened nose. Even at eighteen, Lori had the innocence of a young child. Sometimes she drove Ginny crazy, but Ginny could never stay mad at her.

Lori tossed another plate. "How could he?" she repeated, this time with a grin.

Ginny lunged for the remaining stack of dishes. "No, don't." She grabbed the bowl from Lori's hand, but Lori wouldn't let go. "Come on, sweetie. Give it to me. You can't smash the dishes. It's not funny. I'm sorry I laughed."

They both let go and the bowl shattered across the floor.

Lori wagged her hands, shifting from foot to foot. Glass crunched.

"Ouch, ouch, ouch," Lori bellowed and plopped onto a chair, grabbing her foot.

Ginny gently peeled off Lori's sock. As soon as Lori saw the blood, her tears started.

"Shh, now. I'll put a bandage on that cut and you'll be fine."

Mom appeared at the doorway, looking ten years older than she had when she'd slipped to her room during supper. The lines of her disease—well, both of them—had carved fatigue in her face, and her thinning hair made her seem skeletal. A faded pink bathrobe hung from her shoulders and her threadbare slippers offered little protection against the broken glass.

"Watch your step," Ginny cautioned as she focused on tending Lori's cut.

Mom teetered and reached a knobby hand out for

a chair. She stared at the mess as if Ginny were again three and had helped herself to a glass from the cupboard.

"What happened in here?" Mom's voice slid through her throat, unanchored and sloppy.

Ginny prayed she didn't intend to shore up with another secreted bottle. "It's okay, Mom. Just a couple of broken dishes." She hadn't yet mustered the courage to confront Mom with the telltale signs she'd tumbled from the proverbial wagon after years of restraint. The small brown paper bags. Breath mints on her night table. Unsteadiness Ginny might otherwise have blamed on the cancer. She couldn't have endured the inevitable denials.

The doctors tried to treat Mom's cancer, but they had no remedy for heartache over a wasted life.

Mom glanced at the clock. "Don't we have to be at the council meeting soon?"

"You don't have to come. The approval process is just a formality."

"Nonsense. Those crooks on the town council will dream up any excuse to deny us the group home we need. All they care about is lining their pockets." She fluffed what little hair she had left. "But those clowns will have a harder time living with their consciences if they have to look a dying woman and her handicapped daughter in the eye."

Ginny's gaze darted to Lori. They never called Lori handicapped. She was special.

Lori hopped from her chair and clapped her hands. "Clowns?"

Mom smiled the special indulgent smile reserved for Lori. "That's right, dear. Except these clowns don't have painted faces. Now you go comb your hair while I get dressed."

Oh great, that's just what Ginny needed. Wasn't it bad enough that the man she'd once loved had happened back into her life, as, uh, Duke? "Mom, do you really think you're in any condition to go tonight?"

The spark in Mom's eyes flickered out. "Why can't you see I'm not that person anymore?"

Because you are. Swallowing the words, Ginny turned away.

Rick's newest lie had dredged up all the old betrayals—his and Mom's. Never mind that a small part of her hoped his heart had leaped to life when he saw her, the same way hers had.

Duke. Yeah, sure. His name might be Floyd for all she knew.

And who knew what kind of trouble he'd brought with him?

At the front of the town's council chambers, Mayor Riley, his double chin tripling, leaned back in his padded leather chair and folded his hands in smug satisfaction.

Ginny sprang to her feet to reiterate a dozen reasons why he should reconsider his veto, but before she could utter a word, Rick's voice rose from the back of the room.

"Mayor, if I may, I'd like to address the council. I'm the foreman on this project."

"Your name?"

"Duke." He flashed a warning glance in Ginny's direction. "Duke Black."

The mayor motioned him forward. Ginny slumped into her seat and prayed he didn't make their situation worse.

"That man looks an awful lot like your Rick," Mom whispered, her words remarkably clear given the way she'd slurred them earlier.

"He is Rick."

"Why's he calling himself Duke?"

"Good question, Mother. Why don't you ask him?"

Lori's face scrunched as she pointed at Rick. "That's—"

Ginny clapped a hand over Lori's mouth. Lori's cheeks reddened the way they always did just before she threw a fit.

Thankfully, no one seemed to notice Mom maneuver Lori out the side door. Rick's velvety tones enraptured the audience, and when the mayor called for a vote, the motion to approve the variance passed with only one opposed.

Rick veered toward Ginny wearing a heart-stopping grin, and she scarcely restrained a sudden urge to throw her arms around his neck. "Thank you," she breathed.

"You can thank me by letting me stay on the project." He gave her a sideways hug and heat rushed to her cheeks as she scrambled to recover her composure. He steered her toward the door. "Deal?"

"What?" She slipped from his grasp before the

allure of his closeness brainwashed her into saying something stupid—like yes. He may have won this battle for them, but they'd survived fine without him up until now.

The instant Rick stepped through the council chambers' main doors, Lori launched into his arms. "Rick," she cried out, her voice echoing in the cavernous lobby.

Ginny glanced around the shadowy lobby, wondering why she cared if anyone overheard her sister's declaration.

Maybe it was the way Rick hesitated and stiffened at her words, as if…nervous?

Ginny must've imagined Rick's reaction to Lori's greeting, because a second later he wrapped Lori in his arms. "Hey, kiddo."

To think not so long ago his arms were the only place Ginny had wanted to be. Rick's comfortable acceptance of her sister had been one of the qualities she had admired most about him. Unlike her other boyfriends, Rick had actually wanted to include Lori in some of their activities, or share a meal with her mom. But that had also made his leaving hurt all the more.

Mom eased Lori from his embrace. "Rick, dear. It's wonderful to see you again. Looking so well. Why don't you come back to the house with us so we can catch up?"

Rick shot Ginny a startled look. Fifteen months had ravaged Mom's body. He probably scarcely recognized her.

His gaze softened and the ache in Ginny's chest deepened. She'd been holding herself together since Mom's diagnosis, but one glimpse at the compassion in Rick's eyes and she could feel herself falling apart. She couldn't let herself tumble back into the trap of letting him close enough to share her pain.

"Mom, I'm sure *Duke* has other things he needs to do."

He grinned. "Not at all. I'm all yours."

THREE

Caught between duty and fleeing as far from Rick as she could get, Ginny stayed in the car while Mom led the way to the front door of their bungalow under the protection of Rick's umbrella. Mom had a way of being happily oblivious to the peeled paint on the windowsills, the split in the porch step and the grass long enough to feed a flock of sheep. But if Ginny followed them inside, she'd be all but laying out the welcome mat for Rick to retrample her heart.

"Coming?" Mom called.

Ginny hit the automatic switch for the window. The gears whirred to no effect. She toggled the switch and the window lurched, stopping three inches from the top.

Leaning over, Ginny pitched her voice through the opening. "I thought I'd pick up groceries. Maybe stop by Uncle Emile's. There's something *important* I need to discuss with him."

"Nonsense, you can do that tomorrow." Mom and Lori disappeared into the house.

No such luck with Rick. He hunched next to her

window until their eyes were level. "I can fix that switch if you like."

Rain dribbled off his umbrella and found its way through the gap in the window.

She rammed her thumb onto the button, but the window wouldn't budge. Not up. Not down. Why couldn't he just go away?

Rick opened the car door and offered her a hand. "You go in and dish up the pie Lori promised me, and I'll take care of this window." Humor lit his eyes, and was that a...a...?

"Are you laughing?" *Laughing*? "Oh, you have some nerve, pal. If you knew what kind of month I've had, you wouldn't be laughing. I can't afford any more car repairs." Not when she needed every spare dime to pay for Mom's medicine.

"Lucky for you I want to help then."

"Hello? I—don't—want—your—help! I want you gone."

She reached for the handle, but Rick hunkered between the door and her seat, blocking her attempt to shut him out. He covered her hand with his, and for one second, maybe two, she lost herself in the warmth. Forgetting the rain. Forgetting her mom and sister waiting inside. Forgetting why she shouldn't lean into his embrace.

Then she remembered who he was, or rather wasn't, and snatched her hand away. Everything he did was an act to get what he wanted.

He stepped back and held the door open. "We need to talk before you have that conversation with your uncle, so how about some hot chocolate to go with that pie?"

"Oh sure, that's exactly what I should give you—like a stray puppy, so you'll stick around. Pul-lease."

A full-blown grin dimpled his cheeks and Ginny bolted for the covered porch before he obliterated her resolve.

On the street, a boxy gray car—like the one she'd noticed trolling the neighborhood earlier tonight—slowed. Come to think of it, the car looked a lot like the one that had been idling outside the town hall. She leaned over the porch rail for a better look and the car raced off.

Suddenly grateful for Rick's solid presence, Ginny glanced toward her car.

Inside, Rick had settled into the driver's seat and his fingers grazed the dove ornament dangling from the rearview mirror, his touch almost reverent. Was he remembering the day he gave it to her?

A soaring dove to remind you God is watching over you when I can't be, he'd said.

How she'd cherished his words. Maybe he did know how special he'd once made her feel. With him, her words sparkled, her dreams grew vivid, her hopes became tangible.

He made her believe she could be more than...

"Ginny?" Lori's frantic call cut through the brick and glass.

Ginny trudged inside and hung her wet jacket on the coat tree.

The sweet smell of hot chocolate hung in the air,

and Ginny didn't know why she was surprised. Mom had always had a chameleonlike ability to transform from a wasted alcoholic to Suzie Homemaker in the time it took a social worker to get from the driveway to the door.

Ginny hurried to the kitchen, picking up scattered socks and shoes along the way.

Lori was digging through the freezer and Mom stood at the stove stirring a pot of hot chocolate. But neither had noticed the crumbs and ketchup smeared across the vinyl tablecloth.

Ginny grabbed a wet rag. Appliances and abandoned mail cluttered the countertops, and thanks to the ripped screen in the window above the sink, the fly strip hanging over the table had no vacancies.

"Where's Rick?" Mom chirped.

"His name is Duke." Ginny traded the dishrag for a knife and jabbed the center of the pie her friend Kim's mom had given them. "How can you trust a guy who changes his name for no good reason?"

"I'm sure he has a reasonable explanation. Why don't you ask him? He'll tell you."

"What makes you think I want an explanation?" Ginny snapped as her insides crumbled like the pastry under her knife. She'd waited for months, hoping he'd come back, but he hadn't, which only proved she hadn't meant as much to him as he had to her. Another reason she needed him off this project.

Rick stood on the Bryson porch waiting to be let in. His damp clothes clung to him like the doubts

Ginny had dredged up. Perhaps he could finesse his way into Mrs. Bryson's good graces. She might be just the ally he needed to convince Ginny to trust him.

The Bryson's front door burst open and Lori tugged him into the living room.

The place hadn't changed much. The bright orange globe suspended from the ceiling cast a cheerful glow over the room. Tattered love seats sat kitty-corner to one another, facing the picture window on one side and a blazing gas fireplace on the other. Homey. Lived in. A haven.

"Rick. Play checkers," Lori pleaded.

In the flowery skirt and snug sweater, she looked like a woman, but inside, she was still the fun-loving girl he remembered. "Call me Duke, okay?"

She pushed out her lips and scrutinized him like he'd grown a second nose instead of a moustache. "You Rick." The wide space between her eyes crumpled, and his conscience took another beating.

"Yes, my name is Rick, but it's fun to pretend. Remember when you used to pretend you were a princess? Well, a duke is like a prince." He took her hand and bowed. "You can be a princess, and I'll be Duke."

As though the orange globe had transformed into a glittering chandelier, Lori's eyes lit and she twirled around the coffee table like a princess in a flowing gown. "Okay, Duke."

Mrs. Bryson watched him with guarded eyes. She'd become a mere ghost of the woman he'd once known, and the yellow cast to her complexion had nothing to do with the funky orange light shade. He should've been here for them.

She must've sensed his concern because her reserve mellowed. "It's cancer." She dropped her gaze. "I am getting better."

"That's good to hear."

Lori elbowed between them and tugged Rick toward the sofa. "Date Ginny?"

"I don't think Ginny wants me back, sweetie."

"Yes, do. She your picture. Me show." Lori skipped down the hallway. Before he could relish her enlightening bit of news, Mrs. Bryson took over the interrogation.

"Why did you change your name?"

"I wanted a fresh start."

"Why are you back here then?"

"It wasn't intentional."

"So you didn't come back for Ginny?"

"I…" *No.* He gulped in a breath. He should've come back months ago. Apologized. Explained.

"I don't want to see my daughters hurt again," Mrs. Bryson said.

"Trust me. Neither do I."

She studied him in skeptical silence; his hope that she'd prove an ally dimmed. "Perhaps you should help Ginny serve the dessert before my princess finds that picture."

Buoyed by the reprieve, Rick paused at the entrance to the kitchen and watched Ginny eviscerate the promised pie. "Your window works."

She spun around, knife raised, blood-red cherry juice dripping over her fingers.

He held up his hands in mock horror. "I come in peace."

She looked from him to the knife, then dropped it into the sink. A faint "I doubt that" vibrated beneath the clatter of metal on metal. She swiped her hands on her apron, leaving red juice smeared across her belly.

"I'm sorry about your mom."

Ginny offered a silent nod and scooped ice cream.

"She told me she's getting better."

"Well, you of all people should know you can't always believe what people tell you."

Ouch. She still knew how to deliver the blindside punch. Add to that the tears in her eyes, and he ached like she'd twisted that knife into his chest.

She shoved a tray into his hands, barricading herself behind four bowls of mutilated pie and ice cream. "Go," she said in the same dismissive tone she'd used that night outside the restaurant.

He set the tray on the table. "I'm not going anywhere."

She yanked mugs from the cupboard and busied herself ladling hot chocolate into them. "I can't do this again. I'm grateful that you won over the town council, but I won't keep your secret any longer."

"Your uncle knows."

Ginny's arm jerked and hot chocolate spilled over the side of the mug.

"I told him yesterday." With Ginny's safety in jeopardy, confessing had seemed more prudent than waiting for her to act. He told Laud they'd been close. He told him about his gang affiliations and how Ginny had stormed out of his life when she found out. He told him how he'd moved and changed his name, hoping for a second chance, but that Ginny turned him down. Then he'd handed her uncle a written resignation. Thankfully, Laud refused.

Ginny glared at him with enough firepower to take out a small country. "He knows what? That your real name is Rick? Does he know you were in a gang, too, or did you leave out that part?"

"I'm sorry I let you believe that."

"*Let* me believe? What's that supposed to mean?"

"The Python member who bumped into me was the kind of guy who'd kill his own mother for selling him out. After the way he leered at you, I was afraid he'd use you to get to me. It was safer to let you go."

"Wow, the story sounds so noble the way you tell it. So let me get this straight. You were in a gang, but you intended to sell them out. And you were afraid I'd get caught in the cross fire. Which makes you a hero instead of a liar?"

"More or less, yes." Only he didn't feel so heroic. "You have to understand that it can be a long, hard road escaping from one's past."

A fact.

The hallmark of a successful undercover cop was stating facts that led a person to the most expedient assumptions.

"Have you escaped?" The soft question reflected the heart of the Ginny he remembered.

"I'm working on it," he muttered. Sometimes he hated this job.

"Look, Rick. Duke. Whatever you want me to call you. I'm glad you're turning your life around. But if you truly cared about me, you would have quit this job when I asked, not manipulated your way into my uncle's confidence."

"Ginny, I—"

"I don't want to hear your excuses. If my uncle hasn't seen fit to fire you, I won't try to change his mind. But…if you do anything to train-wreck this project, I will never forgive you. Never."

At the thought of the inevitable fallout following Laud's arrest, Rick's insides piled up like colliding boxcars. "I promise you, your uncle has nothing on me that will derail this project."

Glass exploded into the room.

Rick shoved Ginny down and shielded her body with his. Heart drumming, he scanned the debris. Seeing a rock, he shot to his feet and glimpsed a youth—baggy pants, dark hoodie pulled low over his head—running through the neighbor's back-yard. "Stay down," Rick shouted, sprinting outside. He chased the kid for half a block. Then the kid just disappeared.

Rick braced his hands on his knees until he caught

his breath. The adrenaline shooting through his body took longer to tame.

From all appearances, the vandalism had been a cheap shot by a bored kid out for some kicks. At least that's what Rick kept telling himself as he walked back to the house. One glimpse at the three Bryson women huddled inside the door, their faces pale, told him he wasn't the only one who needed to be convinced.

"I saw the kid, but he got away," Rick said, stepping inside. "I'll clean up this mess and replace the window for you first thing in the—"

Ginny's horrified gaze dropped to a piece of paper crumpled in her hand. Rick swallowed the last of his words.

This was no prank.

FOUR

Unable to stop trembling, Ginny could only watch as Mom soothed Lori's whimpers. *Lord, help me to help them. Give me strength.*

Rick rummaged through the kitchen drawers.

"What are you doing? Don't you want to read the note?"

He pulled out a plastic bag and then carefully clasped the corner of the paper scrunched in her hand. "The police may be able to lift fingerprints. I don't want to add more."

As if she might take back her own fingerprints, Ginny swiped her hand down her shirt. A tangled clump of string slipped to the floor like the sinking awareness she couldn't undo her mistake.

Rick dropped the note into the bag, using the plastic to smooth the paper flat.

Two words scrawled in red ink screamed at Ginny all over again. *I know.*

Rick flipped over the bag, but from the way his jaw clenched he hadn't known another message was scrawled on the back.

One way or the other, HE WILL PAY.

Lori let out a ragged sob.

Rick shooed Mom and Lori out of the kitchen. "Don't worry. Whoever threw that rock clearly had the wrong house."

Desperate to stop shaking, Ginny grabbed the broom.

Rick's attention jerked toward her. "No." He took the broom, curled his arm around her shoulder and drew her away from the debris. "The police will want to see everything as it is. Did you notice anyone suspicious hanging around the area this evening?"

"The car."

"What car?"

"A boxy gray car. It skulked past when you were fixing my window switch. I've seen it before, too."

"Why didn't you tell me?"

"I wasn't talking to you!"

Rick led her to the phone and dialed 9-1-1, but even with his strong arm secured around her shoulders, she couldn't stop shaking. Maybe because his detailed answers to the dispatcher's questions reinforced her growing realization of how little she knew him. One minute he was hanging with gangs. The next he was taking charge, making her want to depend on him.

Gangs. She shrank from his hold, snatched up the note and thrust it toward his chest. "This was meant for you, wasn't it? Wasn't it?"

He glanced at the hole where the kitchen window

used to be and motioned for her to lower her voice. "Why would you think that?"

"Because no *he* lives in this house. And *you* were the one standing in my kitchen when the rock came through the window."

"But the 'he' in this note could refer to..." He hesitated. "Anyone."

"The note says 'I know,' as in I know your secret. How did you think you'd get away with pretending to be *Duke* in this town?"

"I'm a construction worker. No one's gonna connect me to a guy you dated over a year ago."

"You are seriously deluded. You know that? Lori blurted your name in the middle of the town hall." Ginny pointed to the glass scattered across the counters and floor. "Look at this mess. Someone besides me and my uncle knows your secret. What does this person want?"

Rick's eyes shuttered.

"What aren't you telling me?"

"Take it easy," he said. "*If* whoever threw that rock heard Lori call me Rick, he might think he holds some power over me, but he doesn't. Your uncle knows why I'm using an alias. Our rock thrower doesn't scare me."

"Well, he scares me. Isn't it bad enough that you railroaded your way back into our lives without a thought to the emotional havoc you'd wreak on...on Lori? You had to go and bring physical danger to our doorstep, too."

"No, never. I would never—*never*—endanger

you or your family." He cradled her face between his palms, begging her to trust him.

Every whisper of love she'd blocked from her mind rushed to the surface. Months of longing, fighting dreams of what might have been, filled her. She stiffened against the onslaught. She couldn't risk letting him into her life again. He was too good at making her depend on him. And too good at letting her down.

"Please, believe me. That note and rock have nothing to do with me."

She pushed his hands away. "Prove it."

The sound of approaching sirens resonated through the room. For a moment, Rick looked as if he might say something, but then his expression hardened. His fists clenched.

"You can't, can you? Because you know I'm right."

"I'm here because I want to help you. I promise you the rock has nothing to do with me. Ginny," he said and the low, intimate pitch of his voice trembled through her. "If you ever cared for me at all, trust me."

She crossed her arms. All she had to do was look at the glass splintered across the floor to know he couldn't be trusted. "No, Rick, that's the one thing I won't do. Ever again."

Standing in the parking lot of the construction site, Rick shook the building inspector's hand. Too bad convincing Ginny to trust him wasn't as easy as convincing the inspector to rubber-stamp the proposed changes. But divulging what he knew about

Laud could've backfired big-time, especially when she hadn't given a second's consideration to the possibility that the "he" in the note might be her uncle. Rick should just be thankful she didn't share her suspicions of him with the local cops.

He flagged the cement truck to a stop and aimed the trough into a basement window.

If he did his job right, Lori would get her group home and he'd keep them all safe from the danger surrounding her uncle. If only he'd found a match for the partial thumbprint forensics lifted from the note. The fact it didn't match Laud's prints or those of any of the cons Rick had sent to jail, or anyone else's in the police database, was a minor consolation.

Rick blew out a breath and focused on the steady swish of cement. Despite what he'd told Ginny's family, he was certain the rock had been meant for them. And since nothing in the note alluded to a beef with the group-home construction, he was ninety-nine percent sure Laud's creditors were the instigators—upping the stakes to convince Laud to pay. But knowing that didn't help keep Ginny safe. Not when she didn't want Rick within ten miles of her.

He massaged the kink in his neck from too many nights sleeping in his truck outside her place. In the week and a half since she'd been on this project, Ginny had managed to get her name and photograph into every newspaper in the region and had even scored an interview on the local cable station to rally support. What part of "keep a low profile" didn't she understand?

If he hoped to keep her out of harm's way, he needed to secure her cooperation, whether she trusted him or not.

His cell phone rang. The caller ID said *private*, which meant Captain Drake. Rick motioned for Phil to take over the cement trough. Then, with a finger in one ear and his phone to the other, Rick put fifty yards between him and his men. "Talk fast."

"There was another fire last night. In Harbor Creek."

Rick balled his hand. Had his preoccupation with Ginny caused him to miss something?

He tore off his hard hat. Obviously, he'd missed something. Laud had been close-lipped the past couple of weeks, but… "Harbor Creek? That makes no sense. Laud's Harbor Creek complex is already half-filled with tenants. Paying tenants."

"The building wasn't Laud's."

"What?"

"You heard me. The fire marshal thinks we have a serial arsonist on our hands."

"We already know that." Rick watched the truck's tumbler rotate and feared his leads were drying up faster than the cement. "Why would Laud burn down someone else's building?"

"I'm not convinced he's our man."

"Oh, he's dirty."

"Doesn't make him an arsonist."

"You saw the files. You know I'm right. Harbor Creek could be a copycat."

Drake blew out a stream of air. "I know Tom was

your friend, but you need to let this go. You've got nothing that will stand up in court."

"No, I'll never let this go." Not as long as Laud walked free, free to destroy another family for his own selfish ends.

Drake's voice took on the steel edge that meant obey or else. "I'll give you two weeks."

Two weeks—Rick needed all of that to finish the group home, then some. He pocketed his phone and walked back to his crew. Half were local family men, but two or three of the others had criminal records. Men Laud might coax to do his dirty work.

Vic, an ex-con Rick once helped send to jail, gave him a curious look.

Two months undercover on Vic's case had netted a warehouse stuffed with stolen high-end car parts and a five-year sentence for Vic—lots of time for a man to stew over who put him there. Heat pulsed through Rick's veins. Just because he'd kept his identity concealed at the trial didn't mean Vic hadn't figured out who sprang the trap.

Rick's mind flashed to the note—*I know.*

No. The rock thrower was too small to be Vic. Rick slapped on his hard hat. Besides, he'd checked on the whereabouts that night of every crew member. Vic had been at the bar on Fifth.

Rick would keep his eye on him all the same. He might be ninety-nine percent certain that Laud's creditors were behind the attack, but until he neutralized that other one percent no one was above suspicion.

After work Rick headed to Laud's office to test

his reaction to the news of last night's fire. The glass structure stood like a giant prism reflecting the orange sun. In addition to Laud's BMW, a gray Buick sat in the lot. Rick grabbed the construction blueprints to give the impression his visit concerned the project and strode toward the front doors.

A short guy, rumpled suit, slicked hair, averted his gaze and hurried out as Rick reached the door. The guy cut across the lawn and climbed into a dark sedan parked down the street.

Rick couldn't make out the license plate.

A new receptionist, Laud's third in as many months, sat at the desk facing the entrance. "Hi, I'm Duke Black, Laud's foreman."

The redhead looked up and Rick's heart stopped for a full two beats.

Her face had hollowed out, leaving her eyes shadowed. And her hair…

The sun glinted off the short spikes like fiery flames. Her hair used to be brown.

A stab of guilt knifed his gut. How could he have let more than a month lapse since his last visit to Tom's widow?

"Mary? What are you doing here?"

"Duke?" A hint of laughter colored the question. "Is that the best name you could come up with?" She shook her head. "You guys always did act like John Wayne wannabes."

"Hey, I use whatever name they give me." He glanced at Laud's closed door and lowered his voice. "You know how it works."

She matched his tone, and something about her—something more than the hair—seemed different. "So you're investigating my boss? What for?"

"Like I said, you know how this works." If she knew who Laud was and why Rick was here, she wouldn't be within a hundred miles of this place.

"Sure, I understand. Let me know if I can do anything to help."

He slanted another glance down the hallway. "You can look for another job."

"Please don't tell me that. It took me two months to find this one. Miller's Bay isn't exactly an employment hub."

"I thought you and Meaghan moved to Toronto."

"We couldn't. My in-laws petitioned for custody and won. At least temporarily."

"I'm sorry."

"They warned me the day of Tom's funeral they'd do it. I know I'm only Meaghan's stepmom, but I never thought the judge would…" Mary dabbed her eyes with a tissue. "I don't know why I'm surprised. Tom's folks never liked me."

Rick wanted to argue, but he'd seen enough of their attitude to suspect she was right. "If there's anything I can do, just ask."

"Thanks. Just so you know, I'm using my maiden name. My references were from before I married Tom."

"Crantz, got it. We can say we know each other from high school. You can answer one question for me. Who was the guy who cut out of here a few minutes ago?"

"Our salesman, Samuel Jones."

At the end of the hallway, Laud's door opened. He rushed toward the exit, glancing at Rick's blueprints as he passed by. "I've no time to talk now. I'm late for an appointment. Mary, lock up when you leave."

"Yes, sir." Mary turned her attention back to Rick. "I was on my way to the diner for supper. Care to join me?"

Rick thought about the leads he wanted to chase down tonight and resisted the temptation to involve Mary, but when she turned hopeful eyes his way he didn't have the heart to say no.

Ginny slowed her car to make the turn into the parking lot of Hank's Diner.

In the passenger seat, her friend Kim pointed to someone coming out the side door. "Hey, isn't that your foreman guy?"

Despite Ginny's resolve to keep her relationship with Rick strictly business, her heart fluttered at the prospect of running into him.

Kim rubbed her hands together a little too gleefully. Dressed in her usual fitness wear with her hair pulled back in a ponytail, she looked like a kid with way too much mischief in her genes. "Ooh, this will be so much fun. We can walk over to him all nonchalant-like and—" Kim grabbed Ginny's arm. "Stop. Don't turn. He's with another woman!"

Ginny punched the gas and sped away. "What am I doing? Why should I care if he's with another woman?"

"Oh, come on. You haven't stopped talking about him since he got to town."

"Complaining about someone is not the same as liking them." Okay, maybe after his hundred and one *courtesy* calls—updates on the investigation and pleas to lay low—had begun to peter out, she'd actually started to miss hearing from him. But all she had to do was picture that rock smashing through her window to remember why she shouldn't.

"Well, it's a good thing you don't want him because some redhead has already snatched him up."

Ginny veered into the next parking lot, turned around and headed back to the diner.

Kim toppled against the car door. "What are you doing?"

"Going to eat. Where we'd planned." She lifted her chin, ignoring the erratic thud in her chest. She couldn't avoid him forever, especially if she wanted to stay in the loop on their investigation. She just needed to resist his charm, and with another woman in the picture and Kim at her side that'd be a cinch.

"You go, girl," Kim shouted, punching the air like the teen delinquents she supervised down at the detention center. "Just play it cool," she added in her coaching voice. "If there's anything serious going on between Duke and the redhead, he'll avoid you like rotten meat."

"Hmm, thanks for that picture." Ginny parked and wiped her sweaty palms down her slacks. Then, wearing a carefree smile she didn't feel but hoped Rick would believe, she wandered toward the pair.

Rick's tan had darkened, and his hair, a little longer now, looked good, really good. He'd lost the moustache, too, which afforded a perfect view of his dimples.

Dimples that, when he turned to Ginny, made her heart do jumping jacks.

Jumping jacks that must've rattled loose a few brain cells because instead of calling to mind the sounds of shattering glass, all she could hear were whispers telling her that maybe he'd told the truth. Maybe whoever tossed that rock at her window had targeted the wrong house. After all, nothing bad had happened since. Maybe Rick had changed.

"Ginny!"

The delight in his voice sent a delicious shiver down her spine. She waved and tried to find a way to meet his gaze that didn't betray the letdown of seeing him with another woman.

"Have you met Miss Crantz?" he asked. "She's your uncle's new administrator."

"Oh, yes." Ginny's voice lifted with that news flash. "We've talked on the phone."

From the formal way Rick introduced the woman, coupled with the intensity with which he held Ginny's gaze, Ginny would've believed there was nothing between the two, until Miss Crantz swatted his arm in the playful way only close friends do.

"You'd think he was introducing his teacher. We've

known each other since high school." She reached out and shook Ginny's hand. "Please, call me Mary."

Ginny smiled. At least she hoped it was a smile because she couldn't think of one intelligent thing to say. And Kim was no help—hanging back, pretending to be absorbed by a text message.

"I'm glad I ran into you," Rick said in a voice as warm and inviting as hot apple cider on a cold winter's day.

Mary glanced from Rick to Ginny to Kim and back to Rick. "I think that's my cue to get going. Thanks for dinner, Duke."

"I've gotta go, too," Kim chimed in.

Ginny grabbed Kim's arm. "What about dinner?"

"Uh…I forgot that I promised one of the teens at the detention center that I'd help…uh…dye her hair. Yeah, that's right, dye her hair. I'm sure Duke will be happy to keep you company," Kim added with a you-can-thank-me-later lilt.

The one-sided quirk of Rick's lips made Ginny's heart cartwheel. She tightened her grip on Kim's arm. "No, you can't go." The last thing she wanted was to be left alone with Rick. "I drove you. Remember?"

Kim waved off the objection. "Not a problem. I can walk. I'm sure you won't miss me."

"No, I can't let—"

Rick tapped her shoulder. "Stay," he said. "We need to talk." Except this time his tone didn't sound so inviting.

FIVE

Rick could've high-fived Ginny's girlfriend for bowing out of her dinner date. Unfortunately, Ginny didn't look half so pleased.

Her blond hair spilled over her shoulders, and he tried to ignore the stab of longing to tangle his fingers in the silky strands. One glimpse of her sweet smile had reignited the embers he'd been trying to bank for two weeks.

Get a grip, Gray. He was here to figure out how the Harbor Creek fire was connected to Laud, not to fan the flames of his attraction to Ginny.

"Are you sure you want to be seen with me?" she gibed. "Someone might figure out who you really are."

He reached into his truck and grabbed a blueprint tube. "I'm the foreman of a project you're fundraising for—no reason for anyone to think there's ever been more between us."

She strode toward the door. "No, why would anyone think that?"

Swallowing a rise of remorse, Rick jogged after her.

Unlike the coffee shops he usually frequented, where people kept to themselves, at Hank's, with its laminated countertops, black-and-white tiled floor and red leather booths, gossip was freely laundered and hung out for everyone to comment on. Tonight, folks chatted about Bob's new triplets, Owen's new stake truck and the fire in Harbor Creek.

Earlier, while Mary pushed food around her plate, Rick had eavesdropped on the latest buzz, hoping someone might drop info that would help him fit together the newest piece of the arson puzzle. He'd turned up zilch.

Rick guided Ginny to a table near the back of the room. "I'm sorry I spoiled your dinner plans with your friend."

"Don't worry about it." Ginny neatly avoided brushing past him by taking the long way around the table. "No sacrifice is too big for this project."

Rick took his seat and figured he'd do well to remember her motto. But when he looked into her eyes, his brain muddled.

"Is this about the saboteur?" she whispered. "Has something else happened?"

"*No!* No." Rick slid a blueprint from the tube he'd grabbed and spread the paper on the table as he grappled for a way to steer the conversation to Harbor Creek. "I had an idea I wanted to run by you. Are you familiar with any of your uncle's other developments?"

She caught the edge of the blueprint before it curled

back. "Other developments? We need to talk about the investigation."

"The police are handling the investigation. We need to focus on the construction." Before Ginny could do more than bristle at his dictate, Rick redirected the conversation. "What do you think about adding cathedral ceilings to the foyer? Give it a more spacious feel, like the reception area in your uncle's Harbor Creek complex."

Her eyes lit up. "Ooh, I love that idea."

"So you've seen the complex I'm talking about?"

"Sure, I wrote the brochures for it, but…" The enthusiastic gleam in her eyes faded. "Are you sure cathedral ceilings aren't too expensive? Uncle Emile lost money on the Harbor Creek project."

"Your uncle must've recouped his losses by now. Those are high-priced business units in Harbor Creek."

"Uncle Emile is too city-minded. He thinks if you price a unit high, and make it look ritzy, people will believe they are getting more for their money and gladly pay."

"You disagree?"

"Only a fraction of the units are rented, which tells me that small-town business owners don't want showy. They want affordability."

But if affordable units weren't available…

What a perfect decoy. Kill his competition's development and woo the clients to his own. Conjecture of course, but with any luck, plausible enough to convince Drake to let Rick keep digging.

"So do you think the ceiling idea is too expensive?" Ginny said.

Rick pretended to study the blueprints. When he grasped on to the idea he hadn't expected her to actually approve. "I'll run the suggestion by your uncle. If we can make it work, I will." Now, if he could just convince Ginny to talk to him about something other than the project, maybe he could regain a little of her trust.

Rick rolled up the blueprint and handed her one of the menus the waitress had left on the table. "What would you like to eat?"

"Was the ceiling idea your only question?" Ginny's assertive tone dropped to an uneasy quaver as she perched on the edge of her seat, one hand on her purse. "Because you don't have to sit through another meal for my sake."

He reached across the table and touched her hand. "It would be my pleasure."

The tinge in her cheeks betrayed a whisper of yearning. "I'm sure you have more important—"

Rick gave her fingers a gentle squeeze. "There's no place I'd rather be."

A snigger from the booth across the aisle snagged his attention. Vic, a cup of coffee at his lips, tipped a pretend hat.

Ginny drew in a sharp breath, her gaze fixed on the snake tattooed to Vic's muscle-bound arm. The same kind of snake worn by the creep who'd latched on to Rick that night outside the restaurant. The same kind of snake that slithered into her dreams and turned them into nightmares.

Ginny twisted her hand free of his grasp.

"Wait. Ginny, please."

She didn't look back. "I'm sorry. I can't do this."

Ginny sped away from the diner, tires squealing.

How could she have let herself be lulled into thinking Rick had changed? Wasn't Mom's downhill slide proof enough that people never really changed?

No wonder Rick refused to discuss the investigation. If he still met up with his old pals, it was only a matter of time before the police turned their sights on him.

Ahead of her, the traffic light turned yellow.

She stomped on the brake. The car slowed, but not enough. Giving the car more gas, she blasted through the intersection on the red.

In seconds, she caught up to the line of traffic ahead of her and touched her brakes to keep from eating a Mustang's rear end. The car didn't respond.

She veered into the passing lane, but closed in on another car too fast.

Her heart jammed in her throat as she leaned on the horn. *Move!*

The Mustang turned at the next side street, and Ginny swerved back into her lane. She pumped the brakes. Nothing. She had *no* brakes.

Shop fronts blurred past her window.

Terrified by the speed the car picked up on the

meager decline, she careened around the corner at the next side street.

This new street was empty, and flat, and with her foot off the gas the car began to slow.

She blew out a breath and, yanking on the emergency brake, angled toward the curb.

A blue ball punched the car's side window. A flash of pink darted in front of the car.

Ginny veered, automatically stomping on the brake, only to hit the accelerator. *No. No. NO.*

The car's back end swung wide.

Heart pounding, Ginny checked her rearview mirror as she fought to regain control. The girl stood frozen in the middle of the street.

Oh, God, I almost killed that little girl. And I can't stop. Show me how to stop.

Suddenly Lake Erie loomed on the horizon.

A cold chill slapped Ginny's body. The shadows shrank away. The sun became blinding.

Oh, no... Oh, no...

As the road sloped toward the water, the car gained speed. She threw the shifter into neutral. But if anything, the car raced faster.

Ginny wrenched the steering wheel. *Oh, God, please, I don't want to die.*

SIX

Screams, her screams, bombarded Ginny's eardrums. Then suddenly her car jerked to a stop. The seat belt cinched her chest and her head whiplashed.

The post she'd hit stood at an odd angle, and the sickly yellow sign that teetered from it said Dead End. Thirty feet beyond the sign, the dark waters of Lake Erie crashed to the shore.

Ginny squeezed her eyes shut and rested her forehead on the steering wheel. *Thank you, Lord, for keeping me safe.*

Someone pounded on her window. A male voice shouted. The door rattled.

She turned her head toward the sound. It took a while for her eyes to focus on the teenaged boy and for her mind to process his question.

"Are you okay?" he asked, his voice muffled by the window.

When he opened her door, the sound of the car's engine cut through the fog in her brain. She pried her hands from the steering wheel and turned off the ignition.

"My…my brakes." She pulled on her keys, but couldn't make her fingers work. "My brakes…failed."

"Oh, wow," the kid said, looking as dazed as she felt.

She should've listened to her mechanic. He'd warned her the brakes needed fixing. But everything on the clunker needed fixing. Lately, her whole life needed fixing and the car had been the least of her concerns.

"Uh, do you want me to call someone?"

Looking at the dove dangling from her rearview mirror, Ginny swallowed the name wedged in her throat.

Rick.

The last person she should want to see again. Yet the memory of his words when he'd given her the ornament—*to remind you God's watching out for you when I can't be*—burrowed into the hollow places in her soul.

"Ma'am?" pressed the pimply-faced teen.

Her gaze traveled up the street behind her to where the girl had darted out. God had watched out for her. *He* was the only person she needed. "Would you call a tow truck for me?"

"Sure. You can wait in the house, if you want."

"I think I need to sit for a few minutes. Thanks."

As she watched the angry waves break onto shore, Rick's voice whispered through her thoughts. *After the way the Python member leered at you, I was afraid he'd use you to get to me. It was safer to let you go.* She shook her head. The idea was ludicrous. Except…

The sneer of the tattooed guy in the diner flashed through her mind. As did the words from the threatening note, *One way or the other, HE WILL PAY.*

Ginny gulped down her rising panic. *No!* Her car was old. This had nothing to do with Rick. Her mechanic would verify that.

Ginny slipped into her bedroom and, leaning against the door, slid to the carpet. She buried her face in her hands and cried. Cried over frightening the girl. Cried over her silly feelings for Rick. Cried over the clunker she couldn't afford to fix.

After a long while, she propped her chin on her knees and stared at the unseeing eyes of the teddy bear Dad had brought her when he came home from Afghanistan for Aunt Betty's funeral. How many times after he left again—after he left for Afghanistan, and then after he left for good, taken out by a roadside bomb—had she sat in this same spot and poured out her heart to the chubby brown bear?

Grateful she now had a Savior to take her troubles to, she started to pray.

Lori's scream pierced the air.

Ginny bolted to her feet and flung open the door.

Outside Mom's room, Lori wagged her hands and shifted from one foot to the other. "Mommy sick."

Ginny pushed past Lori into the room where Mom was half out of bed, vomiting into a bucket.

"Mommy die," Lori screamed and ran from the room.

Ginny helped Mom to the bathroom and wiped her face with a cloth. Again she began to heave and dropped to her knees in front of the toilet, the spasms that clenched her muscles painfully visible through her thin nightgown. Ginny stroked the hair away from Mom's face.

In all the years Ginny had witnessed Mom's hangovers, she'd never been sick like this. "Did you take your medicine?"

Mom nodded and laid her head on the cold porcelain rim.

"You know you can't have alcohol with those pills."

Mom scowled. "I didn't."

As Ginny rinsed the cloth, her thoughts trickled back to long ago days, before her aunt died and Mom took up drinking. Like the day they went to the carnival and Ginny pigged out on cotton candy. Mom had told her she'd be sick, and later that night she was, but Mom had rocked her and sang her songs and Ginny hadn't minded being sick at all.

Mom retched again and the hazy memory slipped away, shadowed by years of coming home to a bleary-eyed mother.

Ginny helped Mom sit on the edge of the tub, then stripped the soiled sheets from the bed. As she carried the bundle to the laundry room, a book flew past her and crashed into a lamp.

Ginny grabbed Lori's wrists. "Stop."

Lori squirmed free and shoved Ginny away. "Mommy die."

"Throwing books won't help Mom."

Lori threw herself onto the sofa and pounded the cushions. "Mommy can't die."

Ginny sat on the edge of the seat and rubbed Lori's back. "Shh, Mom's just sick. We all get sick sometimes. It doesn't mean—"

Lori's fist flew up and caught Ginny in the cheek. She jerked back, her eyes tearing.

"Ginny?" Mom's weak voice drifted into the room.

Ginny hurried back to the bedroom while behind her something else smashed. She grabbed her cell phone from her room and hit redial. Kim would know what to do with Lori.

Rick's steady voice cut through the clatter and caught her off guard. She forgot she'd called him for an update after making dinner plans with Kim.

Lori screamed and Ginny cupped the phone to her mouth. "Rick, I need you…" Her heart thumped. "Um, I need you to…call my uncle. Send him here right away."

"What is it? What's wrong?"

Glass shattered. "Oh, please, just do it."

From the sound of the glass he'd heard over the phone, Rick had a bad feeling their rock thrower had returned. He broke the speed limit hightailing to Ginny's house and arrived in under five minutes— less time than it might've taken to call Laud, if he'd wanted to, which he hadn't.

Mrs. Bryson's car—the thing had to be older than Ginny—sat in the driveway, but not their Impala.

Was he too late?

Rick grabbed his gun and reconnoitered the perimeter. The living room drapes were drawn. No sign of forced entry. He slowly pushed open the unlocked front door.

A broken lamp and scattered magazines littered the living room. To the right, the bedroom doors were all closed. The sound of breaking glass exploded from the direction of the kitchen.

"Not die," Lori screamed.

Holding his breath, Rick pressed his back against the wall and peered around the corner.

Lori stood in the center of the kitchen, hand held high—a plate clutched in her fingers.

The tension drained from Rick's limbs. He stuffed his gun into his leg holster and stepped into view. "Don't you dare break that."

Lori startled and the dish slipped through her fingers as she hurtled into his arms. "Rick!"

He lifted her away from the broken dishes, and deposited her in the dining room—the only room unscathed by her rampage. "What's going on?"

"Mommy sick."

"Where's Ginny?"

Lori pointed to the bedrooms.

Chances were good Ginny wouldn't be happy that he'd come in her uncle's stead, so he checked the urge to go to her. He squeezed Lori's shoulders.

"Why are you making a mess? You're too old for temper tantrums."

A tear dribbled down her chin. "Noise. Mommy come." Lori's voice hitched on a sob. "No come."

"But I came to see you," he said, doing his best to sound both consoling and firm. "And I don't like messes, and your mom doesn't either. So how about you help me clean this up for her?"

Lori jutted out her bottom lip, but at his disappointed look, she said, "Me sorry."

"I know you are, but Ginny works hard to take care of you. You shouldn't make messes."

"Me work. Me sweep."

After they swept the kitchen, they moved on to the living room. Rick found a bundle of abandoned bedsheets and put them into the washing machine. From the smell, Mrs. Bryson had apparently had a nasty reaction to her treatment.

"Me hungry," Lori said.

"Didn't you eat supper?"

"Cereal. Mom sick. Ginny late."

"Then let's see what we can find." He opened the cupboard next to the sink and a stack of papers tumbled out. Electricity bills. Phone bills. Property tax bills. All overdue.

His heart tripped. How long had they been struggling to make ends meet? He bundled the papers together and shoved them back into the cupboard. From the dates on the bills, they'd been failing miserably for more than a few months.

"Chili," Lori chirped, breaking into his thoughts. "You remember my chili?"

She pulled a tin of beans from the cupboard. "Like chili."

He laughed—a laugh filled with memories of weekends in the kitchen with Ginny concocting outrageous combinations of food, but none as peculiar as the birthday cake Lori had made for him. When the bottle of whipped cream she'd been using to ice his cake had run dry, she'd thought the picture on the aerosol tin in her mom's bathroom looked like the same stuff. He worked his mouth, still able to taste the lemony-scented shaving cream. "Okay, chili it is."

Together they chopped veggies, browned beef and mixed the ingredients. Lori taste-tested each step of the way. As her sweet and chatty nature returned, he reminded her to call him Duke. "How about we play a game of checkers while the chili's cooking?"

Lori's unique version of the game never took long. He had hoped the aroma of cooking food would draw Ginny out of the bedroom. He'd never fully appreciated how much she did for her mom and sister. She was an amazing woman. She deserved to see her dreams fulfilled—like this group home for Lori.

"Checkers, Duke," Lori announced and dumped the box onto the kitchen table.

The sound of his alias rolling so naturally off her tongue pinched at his chest. He caught a runaway checker and sat down to play the game.

This much he could do for Ginny.

He should be following up on the Harbor Creek fire, but he shoved the thought to the back of his mind.

Ten minutes into the game, quiet footsteps moved toward the kitchen. He'd been counting the minutes since he'd arrived, hoping to have time alone with Ginny, maybe convince her he was nothing like the tattooed guy she'd seen at Hank's tonight.

"Rick?" Ginny's cheeks flamed. "What are you doing here?"

"I was worried about you. Is your mom okay?"

Lori twisted out of her seat. "Mommy okay?"

"Yes, she's resting." Ginny smiled at her sister, a smile that awakened a feeling inside Rick he hadn't felt in a very long time.

He went to the stove to stir the chili and gather his simmering emotions. But the instant Ginny moved out of the shadows, a kick of fear swiped his breath. He closed the distance between them and lifted his hand to her bruised cheek. "What happened?"

She winced at his touch and the storm in his chest turned hot and thick.

"I got a little too close to Lori."

"Has this happened before?"

"No." Ginny shrank back at the alarm in his voice. "Not like this."

The implication that it had happened before heightened every last protective instinct. He slid his hand through her hair to cradle the back of her neck and draw her into his arms, but she slipped from his grasp.

"Lori was scared," Ginny explained, her tone defensive. "She hasn't seen Mom that sick before. Most days Lori is happy. Right, Lori?"

"Happy," Lori repeated, tossing checkers into their box.

Ginny lifted the lid from the chili pot and inhaled. "Mmm. Thanks for this and…everything."

"Ginny, I—"

She clopped down the lid. "Let's not go there tonight. Okay?" She sounded beyond exhausted. The phone rang and her shoulders sagged. "Could you get that?"

"Who is this?" Laud demanded from the other end of the line when Rick answered.

"Duke Black. Good evening, sir."

"Where's Ginny? Is she okay?" Laud blurted as if he too had received her frantic call.

But he hadn't, so… "Why do you ask?"

"Because it's not every day a man answers my niece's phone. Why do you think?"

Shadows colored the tender skin around Ginny's eyes and she moved from the stove to the phone as if she were wading through water.

"She's right here. Would you like to talk to her?"

"That's okay. I don't want to interrupt your evening. Will you be there long?"

"Awhile yet, but it's no trouble, sir."

"No, no. The girl needs a social life. Tell her to call

me in the morning." He hung up without waiting for Rick's reply.

After Rick relayed the message, Ginny thanked him for fielding the call. "I didn't feel up to dealing with more questions tonight," she added.

Rick nodded, but planned to ignore the intimation that she didn't want *him* prying either. Laud's call had been a grim reminder that Rick had a job to do. If the Harbor Creek incident was any indication, he'd failed to gain Laud's confidence. Gaining Ginny's might go a long way to remedying that problem.

By the time dinner ended, Rick hadn't made any headway in the trust department. The soft look in Ginny's eyes when he wiped stray chili off Lori's cheek told him Lori was the key to securing an excuse to spend more time with them. Time that would deepen Ginny's trust. Forget that when he sent her uncle to prison, she'd feel betrayed. If putting her uncle away saved lives, Rick was willing to pay the price.

He carried the dirty dishes to the counter. "I noticed a T-ball schedule on the fridge for Lori's team. I'd like to help coach if I may."

"I'm the coach."

"That's why I offered."

"Thank you, but I don't need any help."

When he lifted an eyebrow, she snatched up a dish-cloth and avoided his gaze. "Tonight was an exception. I do appreciate your coming, but I don't need rescuing."

"Who said anything about rescuing?" He smiled

at her reflection in the new window over the sink. "I love sports. You know that."

"I'm sure you're much too busy."

Wasn't that the truth? But the zeal of the special-needs kids had always been a welcome change from the attitudes he faced on the streets. "Trust me, compared to all the hats you're wearing these days, adding a baseball cap to my head a couple of nights a week is no hardship."

Not to mention it would make keeping his eye on her a whole lot easier.

"Those kids need coaches they can count on," Ginny argued.

The pain in her expression drew a groan from deep inside him. Rick brushed the hair from her shoulder, letting his fingers linger. "Ginny, I'm sorry I hurt you. I honestly thought letting you go was for the best. Not a day went by that I didn't miss you, didn't regret that choice."

A tear slipped down her bruised cheek.

His heart squeezed painfully. The last thing he wanted to do was hurt her again. "Let me do this for you. For Lori," he whispered, trying not to notice how her lips glistened, tempting him to taste their sweetness and savor memories of the love they'd once shared, the love he longed to rekindle.

"If I do, you better not let Lori down."

"I won't." He brushed his thumb across Ginny's lips.

She stilled. The look she gave him, as if she longed

to peer inside his head, or maybe his heart, and confirm his sincerity, unraveled his self-control.

His heart thundered as he curled his arm around Ginny's shoulder and drew her closer. "I promise I won't let either of you down." He dipped his head and her lavender fragrance invaded his senses, deepening his desire to seal his promise with a kiss.

The squeal of tires and crunch of metal—courtesy of Lori's TV show—cut his intention short.

Rick jerked back. The image of the revenge-driven crash that took his father flashed through his mind. What was he doing? He had no business dreaming of a future with Ginny.

But how was he supposed to heed the warning screaming in his head when Ginny reached out to him with those green eyes awash with uncertainty?

His cell phone beeped.

Rick wanted to ignore the call and draw Ginny back into his arms. Instead, he gave her an apologetic smile and opened his phone. "This better be important," he growled.

"Buddy, you're in serious trouble."

SEVEN

Ginny curled into a corner of the sofa and tried to follow Lori's TV show. For a breathless moment, she'd felt sure Rick would kiss her, and if the half-dozen apologies he'd made between the kitchen and front door were any indication, her disappointment when he didn't had been plastered across her face.

He'd looked right at home stirring chili at the kitchen stove, in work boots, jeans and a grubby T-shirt—a T-shirt that displayed his broad back and muscled arms too well. She touched her bruised cheek, remembering how the rasp of his fingers had made her skin tingle and how the caress of his gaze had made her insides turn to marshmallow.

The man had even washed the dirty sheets. How could she not care for him?

She buried her face in the cushion and moaned. She didn't want to care for him. Agreeing to let him coach had been exactly the wrong decision. When she should've been remembering the guy with snake tattoos plastered on his arm or the threatening note delivered via rock mail, all she'd thought about was how no one besides Rick knew why she giggled every time she saw a cake covered in whipped cream.

Lori flicked off the TV. "All done."

"Bedtime then." Ginny pushed off the sofa and ushered Lori down the hall.

"Me do," she said, arching away from Ginny's touch.

The phone rang and Lori sprang past her, toward the kitchen.

Ginny caught her shoulder. "I'll get it. You get ready for bed."

Lori's face reddened, but she stomped toward her bedroom.

Apparently, Rick was a better influence on her than Ginny thought. She reached the phone on the fifth ring. At the sound of her mechanic's voice, the terrifying moments before the car crash spiraled through her mind, vivid and raw. Her hands began to tremble, her legs too, even her insides. She sank into a kitchen chair.

What if the girl's ball hadn't punched the car's window? What if she hadn't seen the flash of pink? What if she hadn't swerved in time?

"Ginny, are you there?"

"Yes." She gulped down the lump that had lodged in her throat. "I'm here. You're working late."

"I didn't want to leave my best customer without any wheels."

Ginny twisted the phone cord around her finger. "Have you figured out what happened?"

"Your brake line rusted through. Looks like you hit a rock and the line snapped."

Ginny's breath escaped in a rush. So the accident wasn't connected to Rick after all. She'd been so pre-occupied by Mom's turn for the worse that not only hadn't she pressed Rick for an update on the investigation, she hadn't even thought to confront him with her suspicions.

"I'm afraid the repair will cost more than the car's worth. The whole underbody is rusted. You'll be into thousands to keep her on the road."

Ginny groaned. She didn't have that kind of money to spare. "Okay, I'll let you know what I decide." She hung up and stared outside into the blackness.

Mom flipped on the light and shuffled into the kitchen looking a hundred percent better than she had a few hours ago. "Who was that?"

"My mechanic." Ginny tucked her hands under her arms to hide the way they shook every time she thought about how close she'd come to plowing down that little girl. "My brake line's shot and he doesn't think it's worth fixing." Ginny skipped the story of how she had to smash into a signpost to stop the car.

Mom pulled a box of bran flakes from the cupboard and a pitcher of milk from the fridge. "What will you do?"

Pleased to see Mom interested in eating, Ginny grabbed a bowl and spoon and set it on the table. "I'd hoped I could borrow your car."

"The license plate sticker is lapsed."

"But you drove it last week."

"I figured the worst a cop would give a dying woman was a warning."

"That's crazy. One ticket would cost more than the renewal."

Mom stared at her bowl of cereal. "The money for my medicine had to come from somewhere."

"I said I'd take care of the bills. Uncle Emile offered—"

"I don't want any more charity from your uncle."

"We need Uncle Emile." Ginny motioned to the cupboard harboring their overdue bills. "We have those to take care of, and now my car and yours."

Mom pointed her spoon at Ginny, flicking milk across the table. "We don't need him." Her eyes blazed with a contempt that was almost palatable.

The motor on the fridge kicked out with a sputter that mocked Mom's words. The place was falling apart around them. They needed Uncle Emile's help more than ever.

Mom shoved aside her untouched bowl and globs of soggy flakes spilled onto the tablecloth. "You don't know him like I do. Nothing's free."

"He's your brother-in-law. He's family. If he wanted something in return, he wouldn't be building the group home for us."

"He owes us that much."

"What are you talking about? He doesn't owe us anything. You're the one who shut him out of our lives for so many years."

Mom pushed back her chair, scraping the metal legs across the linoleum. "Where's Lori?"

"In bed." Ginny nudged the bowl toward her mom. "Try to eat something."

"I was happy before Betty died," Mom said, her gaze unfocused, her voice far away.

"I know, Mom. But the fire wasn't Uncle Emile's fault."

"I don't want you asking that man for help."

"Are you hearing yourself? *You* asked him to build the group home. He likes to help. It's who he is."

Mom pushed to her feet. "I'm amazed you don't see it. You are so quick to assume the worst about me. Asking me if I had a drink when I'm retching my guts out! And you assume the worst about Rick, too. You haven't got a clue what kind of man you let walk out of your life. So, what I can't figure out is where the rose-colored glasses you see Emile through came from."

"There are things about Rick you don't know." Ginny balled her hands, fighting to keep her frustration in check. "And you've got to admit, you don't exactly have a history of being honest with me. As for Uncle Emile, he's never let me down."

The fridge motor kicked back in and the lights dimmed under the extra load. Mom flipped off the lights, plunging Ginny in darkness, and stalked away.

"Don't you think it's about time you took responsibility for your own choices?" Ginny called after her.

Mom spun around. The numbers on the microwave clock cast an unnatural green glow to the side of her face. "Yes. I do. That's why I don't want his money."

"Well, I need a car. And there's no way the bank

will give me a loan. So I have no choice. I'm calling Uncle Emile in the morning." Then she'd deal with Rick.

Spooked by Zach's call, Rick circled Miller's Bay one last time to ensure no one had tailed him before heading for his real home. Hopefully, the break-in was nothing more than a coincidence. If it wasn't, he hated to think what it meant.

His headlights cut through the darkness and skittered across the surface of the lake.

The water appeared calm.

Deceptively so.

The undertow had claimed more than one unwitting swimmer, and if Rick wasn't careful this case might do the same to him. When he rushed off without an explanation, Ginny's stricken expression had churned up a mixture of guilt and longing that ran so deep, the weight threatened to suck him under.

He should be happy that she'd let him back into her world, like he'd wanted and needed. Instead, he felt like pond scum.

Rick pressed the accelerator. *Lord, I owe it to Tom to see this case through. Mary deserves justice. She's lost too much—first her husband and now her stepdaughter. But every time I see Ginny, and withhold...* Rick's conscience chafed at the euphemism. *Yeah, okay, every time I have to lie to Ginny, part of me dies. I don't want to give her up again. I'm supposed to be the good guy here.*

Words that had haunted him for fifteen long

months echoed through his mind. *I can't love another person who lies to me,* Ginny had told him.

Lord, what am I supposed to do? The lies are part of my job, a character I play, like an actor.

Silence.

An actor, right. So why did his heart spend half its time wrestling with his brain?

Rick had no doubt Laud torched buildings for profit, maybe even for pleasure. He just wished he didn't have to sacrifice Ginny's dream to prove it.

Tonight, for the first time, he'd witnessed how much she needed a safe haven for Lori. Could her uncle be cruel enough to dangle the group home in front of them then snatch it away for his own greedy ends?

Lord, I can't walk away. Not from Ginny. Not from this case. Please help me be Your man, a man of honor. Show me the way through this.

A ship appeared on the horizon, its lights blazing a path across the dark waters, as if God were saying, *Yes.*

Fifteen minutes later, the swirl of cruiser lights greeted Rick at his house outside Miller's Bay. He parked beside Zach's truck and scanned the perimeter.

A few gawkers lined the street, while inside lights blazed from every room, affording them a perfect view. Zach stalked past upturned furniture toward the door and summoned Rick in. "It's about time you got here."

"Good to see you, too." The place looked like the

eight o'clock train had jumped the rails and barreled through his living room. Rick strode to the window and snapped the curtains shut. "What happened? Who called it in?"

"Lady next door. Grady's interviewing her now."

Rick nodded. Before going undercover he'd been to hundreds of scenes like this, but he'd never felt so violated.

"This kind of vendetta is exactly why I let Ginny walk away from a life with me." He thrust a broken chair leg against the wall. Losing one person he loved to a vindictive criminal had been more than enough.

"Slow down. We don't know if the suspect knows you from Adam. A neighbor saw a kid running down the street around the time of the break-in. This could be nothing more than the lashing out of a drug addict who didn't find the quick cash he'd expected."

"Yeah, right, if you believed that, you wouldn't have warned me to lose any tails before I left town. Thank God whoever did this tracked me to this identity, not Duke." The rest of the thought turned to paste in his mouth. "This kid the neighbor saw...what did he look like?"

"Baggy pants, hooded sweatshirt, short and fast. He was running, not jogging, that's why he caught your neighbor's attention."

The rock thrower. Rick closed his eyes and wished he'd stopped at the lake and dove in the icy water and swam until his muscles screamed, to feel anything besides this fist squeezing his heart. "Anyone see anything else? A car, maybe?"

"Yeah, the guy on the corner said he saw a gray car parked on the side street. Said he'd never seen it in the neighborhood before."

"A boxy car?"

Zach's attention zeroed in on Rick. "Could be. It was an older model."

Rick heard a groan, hollow and tormented, and realized it was his own. He'd brought his troubles to Ginny's doorstep, just like she'd accused.

Scraping his hand over his jaw, he cleared his throat. "Any suspects?"

Zach straddled the only kitchen chair not broken in a dozen pieces. "You tell me. From the sickened look on your face you've obviously got someone in mind."

"Two weeks ago, a kid fitting our runner's description threw a rock through Ginny's window. Someone in a boxy gray car had cased the neighborhood earlier in the evening. The note attached to the rock said, 'I know. One way or another, he will pay.'"

"And you didn't report it?"

"Of course I reported it. I called in the local cops and I informed Drake. I was convinced the note was from Laud's creditors."

"Any proof?"

"No."

"Still convinced?"

Rick paced the room, not wanting to admit that the rock incident and even the attack at the construction site might have been directed at him. "Since when do you handle break and enters?"

"Since tonight. Answer the question."

Rick waited for the tech guy to finish taking pictures and leave. He knew he shouldn't take out his frustration on Zach. His friend wanted to nail the jerk responsible for this as much as Rick did. "I don't like coincidences."

Zach flipped open a notebook. "Okay, let's assume for a minute that the two incidents are unrelated. Where were you tonight?"

"At Ginny's."

"Who knew?"

"What does it matter? I haven't been here in two weeks." Rick scooped a handful of beans from his slashed beanbag chair and watched them slip through his fingers—like the bad guys he put behind bars, only to be sprung by lawyers before breakfast. "Whoever trashed this place didn't have to wait until I was otherwise occupied."

"Sure, a vacant house is an easy target. But you don't think this was the work of an opportunist any more than I do. So we have to assume the suspect picked tonight for a reason. Who's made threats against you recently?"

"Are you kidding me? Who hasn't? Every thug I arrest threatens to make me pay."

"Any you'd take seriously?"

"Trust me, I take them all seriously." Despite the lighthearted tone Rick injected into the comeback, Zach's look of sympathy told him his friend understood how gut-wrenchingly true the statement was. He'd been with Rick the night they'd found his mom and dad trapped in their mangled car—the victims of a deliberate hit-and-run, courtesy of the mob boss that dad's testimony would've put behind bars.

Zach's tone sobered. "I suggest you lay low for a while."

Rick slammed his foot into the beanbag chair. "I'm in the middle of a case."

For the past six years, he'd been operating on the belief that if he worked hard enough, dug deep enough, sacrificed long enough, he could quell the ache of his parents' death, maybe even convince himself that what he did for a living actually made a difference.

Because if he quit, then the bad guys really had won. And he'd promised his dad he wouldn't let that happen.

"What progress have you made on the case since Ginny came on the scene?"

"Proof of minor fraud. A possible motive for the Harbor Creek fire."

"That's it?"

"This is not a quick in and out job where you spend more time doing the paperwork than actually being undercover. I have to gain Laud's trust. I've convinced Ginny to let me help her coach Lori's T-ball games."

"Are you sure that's wise?"

"No, not if some punk keeps throwing rocks at me, but I can't back out now. If I can win Ginny's trust, her uncle will have all the more reason to confide in me."

"Did Laud know you were at Ginny's tonight?"

"Yeah, but—"

"No buts. You told him you changed your name. That's going to make him curious."

"Sure, but this…" Rick motioned to the shredded sofa cushions, the mangled paintings, the toppled lamps. "This is personal."

"Or a clever diversion so you won't suspect Laud's behind it."

The theory resurrected the memory of Laud's cryptic question on the phone tonight—will you be there long?—as if maybe he wanted to know how much time he had. "If he's fingered me, why wouldn't he just fire me?"

"Maybe he hasn't decided whether he can trust you yet. Maybe he's making sure you are who and what you claim to be. Would our intruder have found anything here that tells him you're a cop?"

Rick scanned the room and mentally backtracked through his movements over the past couple of months. "No, the place was clean."

"Sometimes *too* clean can be just as telling. People who don't have something to hide will have a file cabinet stuffed with old tax returns, receipts, an address book, photos."

Rick's gaze flicked to the end table where a photo of him and Tom had sat. Rick tossed sofa cushions aside, checked under furniture. Nothing.

"The photo of Tom and me is gone," he growled, the roar of his own idiocy felling every last defense he'd made for staying on this case. The attacks had to be connected. Drug addicts and vindictive ex-cons had no reason to steal a photo.

"Were you in your uniforms?"

Rick slapped the cushion back on the sofa. "No."

"So nothing that would give away that you're a cop?"

"If Laud's behind this little house inspection, that photo is all the proof he needs to figure out that I have ulterior motives. Tom's picture was plastered all over the newspapers after the town house fire."

"Okay, but we don't *know* that Laud's behind the break-in. I'll need a list of everything that's missing, everyone who's made threats against you. Recent cases. You know the drill."

Yeah, he knew the drill. And he didn't have time for this. He straightened the one painting that still hung on the wall, tugged his recliner back on its feet and groaned at the knife slash across the leather cushion. Wires dangled from the wall. "The TV is gone."

"You'd better look around the rest of the house."

Rick stopped at the entrance to his bedroom. The TV wasn't stolen. The slime had plugged it in and tossed it onto the sliced waterbed.

Electrocution. *Nice.*

"Since you and Ginny have a history," Zach said quietly, his expression sober, "if Laud's figured out you're a cop, he'll never believe Ginny didn't know. He'll assume she betrayed him."

Rick's stomach tightened, the way it did when he hit a patch of icy pellets on the road, felt the skittering looseness under the tires and knew he was nanoseconds away from spinning out of control. Instead of protecting Ginny, he'd endangered her more than ever.

EIGHT

When Laud motioned Rick into the portable on-site office, a slow burn ignited in the pit of his stomach. If Laud was behind last night's break-in, Rick had about ten seconds to concoct an explanation to counter whatever conclusions he'd drawn, especially where Ginny was concerned.

Laud took a seat behind the desk. "Shut the door."

Rick nudged it closed with his foot.

"I assume you and my niece mended your rift?"

"I'm working on it, sir." If Laud wanted to take the long way around this conversation, Rick was happy to oblige. He leaned against the wall, crossing one foot over the other, giving away nothing.

"Did she mention her accident?"

"Accident?" Rick's breath scraped against his ribs. "What accident?"

"Her brakes blew. She thinks they rusted out, but I have my doubts."

"You think someone tampered with them?" Then it had to be connected to the other incidents. If

Laud wasn't behind them, someone bent on revenge wanted Rick to bleed in the worst possible way.

"Yes, and I want you to find out who."

"Me? Why me?"

"If you and Ginny are rekindling your relationship, she won't question your sudden interest in her well-being."

Rick liked the sound of that, although if he found the guy, he might not be able to stop himself at beating him to a pulp. "Do you have a particular suspect in mind?" He had a long list of people who might be after him. Starting with Vic.

Rick squinted through the window at the man on the roof. The Incredible Hulk wannabe hadn't betrayed a hint of recognition when he'd introduced himself to Rick on his first day of work. But he'd shown an unnerving interest in him and Ginny at the diner…before her accident.

The scum must've been following him, waiting for a mark.

"In my line of work one makes an enemy or two." Laud handed Rick a slip of paper. "These are a few names. I thought, given your past, you might find out if anyone is talking."

Rick would've grinned at the request that brought him one step closer to Laud's circle of trust. *Would have,* if Ginny's life weren't at risk.

When Ginny's ride deposited her at the curb of the construction site, anxiety radiated off of Rick like heat at a three-alarm fire, which meant something else must've happened. Ginny hurried toward him and Uncle Emile. Another sabotage incident would explain why Rick had rushed off last night. And if she hadn't volunteered to meet Uncle Emile here for their car shopping trip, they probably wouldn't have informed her. "What's going on?"

"I'll wait in the car," Uncle Emile said.

Rick pulled Ginny aside, and her heart tripped at the intensity of his gaze. "Why didn't you tell me that your brakes blew?"

"My brakes?" She blinked. "You mean last night? I was a little preoccupied with my mom."

"Have you had trouble like this before?"

"Brake trouble? Is that what you're brooding about? The car was old. Everything was failing."

"Did you notice any leaks? Drips in the driveway?"

The urgency in Rick's voice rattled her. "No."

"Sponginess in the pedal?"

"No," she said, louder this time. She felt horrible enough for frightening that poor girl. She didn't need to be reminded that if she'd been more attentive to her car's maintenance she might've prevented the accident.

Rick squeezed her hand. "I'm sorry. I didn't mean to upset you. With everything that's been going on, I kind of freaked when Laud told me what happened."

"It was corrosion," she assured him, although his allusion to her own initial fears knocked her heart into an uneasy rhythm. "My mechanic confirmed it."

Rick nodded but didn't look convinced.

"What aren't you telling me?"

The telltale muscle in Rick's cheek flinched. "That call last night... There was another incident."

"I knew it." She scanned the construction site for damage. "You should've told me. I would've come with you."

"I don't want you involved."

Ginny planted her hands on her hips. "It's too late for that. Don't you think?"

Rick felt like Ginny had scooped out his insides and left them for the birds to scavenge. He'd downplayed his fear that she'd been targeted so as not to scare her, but the moment she left, he headed to the mechanic's, phoning Zach on the way. "We have a new problem."

"What's up?"

"Someone sabotaged Ginny's brakes. I want her under twenty-four-hour surveillance."

"Whoa, slow down. Do you think the sabotage is connected to the break-in?"

"Think about it. If someone wants to get back at me, what better way than to threaten someone I care about?" Rick turned into Ed's parking lot and scanned the street. "I don't like coincidences."

"I can't requisition surveillance on someone because you don't like coincidences. When did this happen?"

"Last night." Rick yanked his keys from the ignition. He'd been so distracted by his desire to win Ginny's trust, he'd completely forgotten to ask why her car wasn't in the driveway. But Zach didn't need to know that. "Laud thinks someone targeted Ginny to get to *him*. He wants me to figure out who. I'll text you a list of names to check into."

Zach whistled. "He gave you names?"

"Yeah. It seems he trusts me. Imagine that."

"You don't sound convinced."

"I'm not. Not completely." Too many things like Laud's out-of-place question on the phone last night didn't add up. "That's why I want someone on him. He's got Ginny. This could be a setup, or a test of my loyalty, or…"

Rick stared at the pole-sized dent in Ginny's front bumper and the words turned to dust in his mouth. "Or someone really wants to hurt her. And I need to know why."

A mechanic emerged from the garage wiping his greasy hands on an even greasier rag. The name embroidered on his blue coveralls was Ed. He ignored Rick's outstretched hand and kicked a crawler toward him. "I don't know what Laud expects you to find. The car is a rust bucket. A crack in the line was bound to happen sooner or later. I warned her."

Rick pulled a penlight from his pocket and wheeled himself under the car. The guy was probably worried about a lawsuit, but he was right. Ginny's car was an accident waiting to happen. Rust flaked off with a flick of a fingernail. Although close to the site of the break, the metal appeared glazed as though it'd been bashed by a rock. A spray of gravel wouldn't do that kind of damage.

Only an idiot or someone with something to hide would suggest an incidental bump caused this breach. Rick's stomach tightened as he mentally added Ed to his list of suspects.

What possible motive would the mechanic have to hurt Ginny? It made more sense that someone paid him to lie.

But who? And why?

If, as Laud assumed, his enemy targeted Ginny as a warning, why make it look like an accident? A saboteur would want them to know the attack was deliberate.

Rick slammed his fist against the car's underbelly and rust flakes showered down on him. Spitting and blinking, he wheeled out from under the vehicle.

Ed strode toward him, a smirk on his face. "Find what you were looking for?"

Rick brushed himself off. "Yeah, thanks." If he could find the rock used to bash her brake line, maybe he could lift some fingerprints. At the moment, he'd like nothing better than to find Ed's fingerprints on the mystery rock and wipe that smirk off his face with it.

Next, Rick headed to Hank's Diner where he found enough rust flakes and stained pebbles in the parking lot to substantiate his theory that Vic was their culprit.

If Rick hadn't let Vic distract his attention, Rick would've walked Ginny to her car and possibly noticed something amiss. Instead, it had been the Snake scene all over again, with the old fears resurfacing that his job might endanger her. And here he was confronting the very thing he'd wanted to protect her from—her life being threatened.

Rick returned to his pickup and checked in with Zach.

"I ran down the names Laud gave you," Zach said. "They're all the type who'd hire punks to do their dirty work."

Like the creeps who'd driven his folks off the highway. Rick ground the gears into second. "Did you contact any of our regular informants? Find out what they've heard on the street."

"I put Grady on it."

"Okay, our best hope of catching this guy is by watching who's watching Ginny. She'll be at the baseball diamond tonight and I want you in the stands."

"Won't you be there?"

You better not let her down, Ginny's words taunted him.

Last night, he'd considered it a personal challenge to win her approval of his offer to help coach. Now, he wished he'd kept his mouth shut. Then he could be the one covertly watching from the stands. "Yes, I'll have the view from the field. But I may be late."

Seven hours later, when Rick caught himself checking the rearview mirror for the twentieth time, he knew he wasn't ready to discard his theory that someone might use Ginny to get to him. Just not Vic.

The man had driven straight home, exited twenty minutes later, in khakis and a crisp white shirt, and walked two blocks to St. Alban's Church—the location of the town's weekly AA meeting. Such a positive step didn't mesh with nursing a vendetta against the cop who sent him to jail.

Rick turned east toward the ballpark.

Zach had better be there because by the end of the night Rick wanted a full report on every person who so much as looked sideways at Ginny.

Frustration wadded in his chest. He intended to do everything he could to avoid looking like he cared about her, because he had no intention of fueling misconceptions that might lure her attacker to strike again. But the feat would test his acting abilities to the limit.

Rick drove past the ball diamond and parked on a side street. Once he was satisfied that no one had followed him, he pulled on his cap and approached the ballpark from the outfield side, scanning the area for anyone who seemed out of place.

A guy with a crew cut cycled by, glancing toward the infield more than once. A trio of women jogged on the track circling the park. The redhead waved. Mary?

Yes, Mary. Rick lifted his hand enough to acknowledge the greeting but hopefully not enough to catch anyone else's attention.

A young mother pushed a toddler on a swing as she watched special-needs kids spill onto the field, many accompanied by a parent or helper. With all those extra helpers, Ginny really hadn't needed his help.

That realization tunneled into his heart and swelled into something warm and soft.

Ginny, her long blond hair looped through the back of her ball cap, handed a red or blue numbered bib to each player. Lori, wearing a blue bib, stood at second base, glove in hand. Zach sat at the top of the stands in dark sunglasses and a Blue Jays cap. Rick jogged across the field toward Ginny. Let the game begin.

Ginny reined in her tumultuous emotions at the sight of Rick jogging toward her. His overprotective reaction to her rusted-out brakes had roused all sorts of warm and fuzzy feelings. But Uncle Emile hadn't known anything about another *incident*, neither had the police, and when she'd gone to confront Rick after buying her car, his lead hand said he'd taken the day off. "Gray, you're late."

He tipped up the brim of his hat. "The name's Black. Where do you want me?"

His cool regard froze the answer in her throat. She'd barked his real name without thinking. But really, who within hearing distance cared?

She slapped the bat into his hand. "You can be the batting coach." If he wanted to be a tough guy, he might as well take the most dangerous position of the game. She smirked, but he didn't rise to the bait.

Two innings into the game, Ginny realized her mistake. Making Rick the batting coach meant she had a ringside seat to the flex of his muscled arms, which only reminded her how special she'd felt curled inside them; to the timbre of his encouraging instructions, which reverberated with last night's promise *I won't let you down;* and even to his scent, a mixture of spice and masculinity that wrapped itself around her like a cozy fleece blanket.

How could she concentrate on the game with Rick constantly distracting her?

His patience with each batter, adjusting their stance, positioning their hands on the bat and perfecting their swing, made her fall for him all over again. And hadn't she told herself she didn't want to do that?

Apparently, he'd gotten the message, because he scarcely met her gaze, even when she shouted instructions to him. In fact, he seemed to look everywhere but at her.

She called for the next batter and told herself he wasn't ignoring her. He was focused on the game, and she was the one who was preoccupied.

With him.

But when the scorekeeper called game and Lori bounded toward him shouting "Come, ice cream?" Ginny knew there was more to his sudden reticence.

Rick's gaze slid to the stands and he tugged the brim of his ball cap a little lower.

When he didn't respond to Lori's invitation, Ginny said, "It's tradition for the team to go out after a game."

"I'm afraid I can't tonight." He started to leave.

Ginny grabbed his arm. "Hold it right there, buster. You have some explaining to do."

"Excuse me?"

"Last night's incident? The police have no record of it."

"You called the police?" Rick chewed on the inside

of his cheek and Ginny could almost see the little mice racing inside his brain, trying to find a way out of this one.

"What did you expect when you sloughed off my questions? If you think I'll sit back and let you cover up whatever is going on, think again."

Rick patted the air with his palms. "Keep your voice down. I'm not sloughing you off. Your uncle was waiting for you this morning. And tonight I have a meeting. As for the missing police report, the incident—a break-in—occurred in another jurisdiction. Believe me, I want to nail this culprit as much as you do." He glanced at his watch. "But I've really got to go, now."

Kim jogged over to where Rick had abandoned Ginny on the field. "What did I miss?"

"Nothing."

Kim flung an appreciative look at Rick's retreating back. "Uh-huh…"

"It's not like that. He helped coach the game. That's all." That's all he'd offered. And that's all she'd agreed to. So why did it bother her so much?

Maybe, because last night, her traitorous heart had replayed his words—*not a day went by that I didn't miss you*—like a broken record, and fool that she was, she'd started to believe them.

Lori pointed to the players climbing into their cars. "Ice cream."

Ginny stuffed down her hurt feelings to deal with later and jangled her keys at Kim. "Do you want to come? I'll let you ride in my new car."

"No way! I leave you alone for a day and you have a new man and a new car?" Kim hooked Ginny's elbow and tugged her toward the parking lot.

"There is absolutely nothing going on between me and *Duke.*"

"Don't worry. I'm sure we can fix that." Kim climbed into the car. "After we get ice cream, we'll go shopping." She turned to Lori in the backseat. "What do you say? Don't you think your sister needs a new outfit to knock the socks off Duke?"

"Socks off!" Lori clapped.

Kim gave Ginny a smug look. "It's unanimous."

"I'm not interested in knocking Duke's socks off."

"Save it for someone who'll believe you. I saw the way you watched him."

Ginny pulled into the Dairy Queen. She knew better than to trust Rick, but when he tousled Tommy's hair after the boy whacked him in the shins with a bat, she found it hard to swallow and her rib cage felt two sizes too small. She wanted to love someone just like him. "For all I know, his new identity is a front for some major new crime spree he intends to spring on Miller's Bay."

Kim burst out laughing. "You don't believe that."

"I don't know what to believe." She'd obviously misread his intentions. So why was she still obsessing over him?

By the time they headed to the mall, Ginny had practically put Rick out of her mind...until a familiar gray car appeared in her rearview mirror.

NINE

Rick snagged the phone vibrating at his hip and withdrew into the shadows of the crowded restaurant, out of earshot of Laud and his newest associate. "It's about time you checked in. Where did you run off to after the game? I need to know what you saw."

"I had another call out," Zach said. "Unlike you, I actually work more than one case at a time."

"Yeah, yeah. What did you see?"

"First you have some explaining to do. Like why didn't you tell me Mary works for Laud Developments?"

"It wasn't exactly on my mind after my house got trashed."

"Does she know why you're working there?"

"No. Why would she?"

"How about because at Tom's funeral you told her you wouldn't rest until you figured out who killed her husband?"

Rick let out a groan that started in the pit of his stomach and twined its way through his chest before finally reaching his vocal cords.

"Yeah, I thought you might feel that way. I told her Drake put you on another case because you were too close to Tom's to think straight."

"Thanks." Wow, it hurt to say that. Not because he wasn't grateful that Zach covered for him, but because he was beginning to think Zach might be right.

"I mean it, Rick. You're not just *playing* with fire. You've tossed in live ammunition."

"Mary won't blow my cover."

Zach's silence chewed up and spit out what was left of Rick's confidence.

"Look, are you going to tell me what you saw at the ball game tonight or not?"

"Nothing. No one paid Ginny any attention."

"No one?" Rick repeated, to be sure he'd heard right.

"Not a one. There were, however, a couple of people *very* interested in *you*."

So his instincts had been right.

"A beautiful blonde with big green eyes. Eyes she couldn't tear away from you the entire game."

"A woman?" Rick's mind zigzagged through the ramifications of that piece of intel. "That explains why none of the names I gave you turned up leads. We need to figure out which convict has a wife or girlfriend angry enough to come after the guy who put her man behind bars."

"Man, you are seriously sleep deprived," Zach said with disgust. "The blonde was Ginny."

"Ginny?" Couldn't tear her eyes off of him?

A jolt of pleasure zinged through Rick's chest. But

the effect lasted only a moment. "You said there were two people."

"The other one was a brunette sitting on the sidelines. She ran over to Ginny the second you walked away. Obviously a girlfriend."

"You're positive there was no one else out there? No one spying from their cars, the playground, the sidewalk?"

"I'm telling you there was no one paying either of you the slightest bit of attention. No sign of anyone in a hooded sweatshirt, or of a boxy gray car. Get some sleep. Tomorrow's search should give us some fresh leads."

Rick let his gaze stray to the restaurant window and the star-filled sky. *She couldn't take her eyes off of me, huh?*

Maybe a future with Ginny wasn't such a lost cause after all.

The minute Ginny got home from the mall, she put in a call to Rick. No guy in a gray car had gone around spying on her before he showed up in town. She wanted answers and she wanted them now.

"I'll be right over," he said. Five minutes later a blast of damp night air and a whiff of skunk followed Rick in through the basement patio door. The fact he'd used the back door rather than the front reinforced Ginny's certainty that he had something to hide.

"It's time you tell me what's really going on." She

threw a glance at the ceiling, hoping Mom and Lori wouldn't hear.

He gave her a blank look, but his silence spoke volumes.

Too bad, too, because she'd started to hope his lines weren't just, well, lines. "Don't play dumb with me. Our friend in the gray car tailed me tonight."

Rick's eyes widened in what could only be described as horror, and she almost felt sorry for him. Almost.

"I lost the creep. Shaking him was actually pretty easy. Although a lot of good it does me, since…" Until this moment, her anger had blinded her to how much danger she was really in. "He knows where I *live*." She snapped the drapes closed and backed away from the window.

"Did you get the license plate?"

"Are you kidding me? I was too freaked out."

Rick winced, actually looked downright sick.

"Why is this person following me? And why does it always happen after I've been around *you*?"

He looked away. "I don't know."

"I think you do."

Rick's mouth pressed into a grim line.

"What is it? Has one of those gang buddies you double-crossed tracked you down?" At his pained expression, her breath caught. "That's it, isn't it?"

"It's possible." He sounded like he'd been punched in the chest and the embattled look in his eye said he blamed himself.

But did he seriously think he could apologize his way out of this?

Suddenly, the suspicion she'd refused to acknowledge became gut-wrenchingly clear. "It's that guy from the diner. The one with the tattoo. After he saw us together—"

"No." Emotion flashed across Rick's face, but his voice was tight. "I checked him out. I don't think he's our man."

"But you don't think my brake failure was an accident?"

He touched her jaw. "Your brake line was bashed."

The floor tilted under her, not from fright but from the way Rick looked at her, heart wide open, as if he'd do anything to change what happened. "You looked at my car?"

"Yes." He circled his hand behind her neck, and it felt so warm and steady and…protective. He'd been looking out for her. Trying to keep her safe. Her heartbeat thrummed against the gentle caress of his thumb. "As soon as I realized that your connection to me might endanger you, I stepped back so the saboteur would realize you weren't anything special to me and leave you alone."

She shrank from his touch. "Hmm, thanks. Nice to know where I stand."

Rick closed his hands over hers and held them against his chest. "That came out wrong." His breath whispered across her cheek. "You are *very* special to me. I just didn't want the wrong people to know how much."

She closed her eyes. Oh, how she longed to believe him. Would she never learn? She yanked her hands from beneath his and put a chair between them. "Clearly, your plan didn't work. So how about you tell me everything you know and we'll deal with this together."

Rick braced his broad hands on the chair back, digging his fingers into the cushion. "You won't like what I have to say."

"I'd rather know the truth than be lied to out of some misguided notion that I'll somehow be happier or safer."

A muscle pulled in Rick's jaw as he groped for words. "Your uncle didn't want to worry you. He's made some enemies and he's afraid they've targeted you to get his attention."

"I don't believe you. My uncle wouldn't get mixed up with people like that."

"He may very well deny it if you ask him. And then fire me for telling you. But why would I lie?" Rick sent the chair rolling to the side and took her face in his hands. "I only care about keeping you safe."

His soft words turned her inside out. His intense drive to protect her was one of the things she'd loved most about him, because all her life she'd been the one doing the protecting.

It had felt good to lean on someone else.

Then he'd left, and the dove hanging from her rear-view mirror became her reminder that she needed to lean on God alone. Except Rick had come back and wanted to be her protector.

Unspoken regrets shadowed his eyes. "I honestly don't know whether some psychotic protester or one of your uncle's enemies or one of mine has targeted you. But I promise you I'll figure it out and put a stop to him."

"*I*? Uh-uh. Whether you like it or not, we're in this together. No more secrets."

He hesitated, then brushed his thumb across her lips, assurance in his eyes. "I like the sound of that."

From the cover of his truck, Rick watched Laud follow Ginny and Lori into Bay Community Church before calling Zach. "You're good to go."

"I don't know why I let you drag me into this case."

"Me? You're the one who insisted on investigating my break-in. A little dumpster diving won't kill ya." Rick pocketed his phone and stretched out the kinks in his neck from sleeping in his truck outside Ginny's house. Her offer of allegiance had dug up all his longings and almost made him confess he was a cop. A cop who'd spent the past few weeks lying to her. Lying to protect her and to nail the bad guy. Her uncle.

Then he'd come to his senses.

He may have said they'd work together, but just enough to keep her out of trouble so he could do his job. This morning that meant somehow convincing

Laud he was in love with Ginny without the entire congregation assuming they were a couple.

It was bad enough one vengeful psychopath already might.

By the time Rick made his way inside, the worship team had mounted the platform. Ginny and Laud sat in the third row on the left. Laud would expect Rick to join them, but his late arrival might justify the lapse. Rick slipped into the back pew on the right.

The place hadn't changed much since the one and only time he'd joined Ginny for a service. He could still feel the warmth of Ginny's hand in his as their voices blended in hymns of praise. He'd never felt closer to God than at that moment. Lately, he felt as if his deceptions had clipped the wings of his faith.

Sure, he could recite line and verse from Scripture, depicting plenty of men who lied for a greater purpose. But more and more, the verses showing God's hatred of lies crowded the others from his mind.

Music filled the sanctuary. The worship band had grown from a couple of guitarists and a pianist to include a drummer, a bass player and…

Lori?

She stood center stage grinning from ear to ear, thumping her tambourine in an enthusiastic, if not rhythmic, interpretation of the song that seemed to please everyone.

When the worship team disbanded to find their seats, Lori spotted Rick and waved even more enthusiastically than she'd played the tambourine. Laud tracked her gaze and pinned Rick with a disapproving frown.

His heart burst into a full-out gallop.

More faces turned his way.

Resisting the temptation to look behind him in the insane hope someone else might return Lori's greeting, he offered a feeble wave. He should have known better than to think he could keep a low profile with Lori here.

Like the rest of the worshipers, Ginny craned her neck to see who Lori had singled out. Except when Ginny's gaze touched his, her eyes lit, and Rick forgot to try and hold out against the smile tugging at his lips. Ginny tipped her head sideways, no more than an inch, and one eyebrow lifted.

He pointed to his watch and shrugged.

When she nodded and Laud's frown receded to a thin straight line, Rick's heart settled into a steadier rhythm.

Thankfully, the pastor snagged everyone's attention back to the front of the room. His hair had turned white since Rick last saw him, probably because his daughter's hair was now a funky purple streaked with orange. Rick scanned the pews looking for anyone who paid more attention to Ginny than to the pastor.

Her mechanic had scrubbed himself as squeaky-clean as his record. The man didn't have so much as a parking ticket, but Rick hadn't missed how his gaze continually strayed in Ginny's direction.

Rick was encouraged to see Mary. After her loss, attending church alone had to be hard.

Rick winked at a baby eyeballing him over her mama's shoulder. If he'd made different choices fifteen months ago, might he and Ginny have a child by now? His throat clogged at the thought. Ginny would make a wonderful mother.

The pastor's words filtered into Rick's thoughts. "Jesus said, 'There is nothing concealed that will not be disclosed, or hidden that will not be made known.'"

How ironic that most people feared those words.

Rick longed for the day he could disclose his true life to Ginny. The day she would finally understand he worked for a greater good. The day she would know he was honorable.

Outside, a dark sedan rumbled into the parking lot.

A woman across the aisle glanced out the window and her face turned ashen. With trembling hands, she gathered her purse and hurried from the sanctuary.

When the sedan's door slammed and the stocky driver marched toward the Sunday School wing, Rick trailed the frightened woman. He rounded the corner a moment before she slipped into a classroom and the man stormed into the building. Rick jogged toward him. "May I help you?"

"Yeah, where's the grade three classroom? I have to pick up my kid."

Rick positioned himself between the six foot, two-hundred-and-fifty-pound man and the classroom where the wisp of a woman had disappeared. "Class won't be over for half an hour. Would you like a coffee while you wait, Mr....?"

The man shoved Rick aside. "I don't have time to wait."

Rick hooked his foot around the guy's ankle. When the man stumbled, Rick caught his wrist and twisted his arm behind his back. "What's your hurry?"

Ten feet away, the woman and a tawny-haired girl scurried down the hall like a pair of frightened rabbits.

Rearing backward, the man crushed Rick against the wall.

Bright colors exploded before his eyes. His grip loosened.

The man jabbed an elbow into Rick's gut and broke free.

A hand shot out from another classroom and yanked the woman and girl inside.

Rick launched himself at the guy's back. "I don't think she wants to see you."

They crashed through the door onto the floor. Rick shoved a knee into the man's spine and grabbed his wrists.

Swearing, the man twisted and kicked.

Wide-eyed children huddled in silent terror behind the protective arms of a lanky brunette—Ginny's friend, Kim.

Pinning both of the man's wrists under one hand, Rick tossed her his cell phone. "Hit redial. Zach's a cop. Tell him to send a car, no sirens."

"You'll pay for this," the suspect shouted, heaving his chest off the ground.

Rick yanked the guy's wrists higher, wrenching his shoulder. "Ready to cooperate?"

"I just want to see my little girl. Don't you have kids?"

From the corner of his eye, Rick spotted the woman and her child edging toward a second exit. Frightened brown eyes raked over him. A faint yellowing around the left was no doubt the remnants of a meeting with her husband's fist.

"It's okay. I've got him." Rick ground his knee into the man's kidney. "He's not going to hurt you."

"I just want to see my little girl," the man moaned.

Kim finished the call and hustled her young charges into an adjoining classroom. Then she wrapped an arm around the trembling mother and child and reiterated Rick's reassurance.

Kim's composure and faith in Rick stunned him. Of course, according to the background check he'd run on her, she was a youth worker at the local juvie home and probably saw more than her fair share of guys like this wife-beater.

"You'll pay for this. You'll all pay," the man fumed.

"Is that a threat?" Rick punctuated the question with a twist to the guy's wrists. "In front of witnesses? I thought cowards like you only made those kinds of threats to helpless women and children behind closed doors."

Two uniformed officers relieved Rick of the scum. After they cuffed the guy and hauled him off the ground, he studied Rick with a scowl, as though memorizing his face.

Terrific, yet another psychopath gunning for him.

One officer escorted the man to the police cruiser while the other officer recorded the wife's statement.

Kim sidled over to Rick and extended a hand. "We weren't properly introduced the other night. I'm Kim. Thanks for being here. I hate to think what might've happened if you hadn't been."

"The name's Duke."

"Yeah, I know. Ginny's boy—, uh, friend. She's told me all about you."

Rick stifled a groan. At any other time, he might've been thrilled to learn Ginny talked about him with her girlfriends. "Listen," Rick said in a confidential tone, "please don't tell people about what happened here."

"Are you kidding me? You're a hero."

Wow, a cop didn't hear that every day. At his last domestic violence case, the wife had started yelling at *him* after he cuffed her husband. But as much as Rick would relish seeing a little hero worship in Ginny's eyes, he couldn't jeopardize her safety. Someone bent on making him pay for putting them behind bars would delight in targeting those closest to him. "It's just that Ginny and I aren't a couple, and I don't want people to get the wrong impression about us."

"Oh." A frown eclipsed the light in Kim's eyes, and Rick had the sinking feeling his explanation had sounded a whole lot worse than he'd intended.

"If you'll follow us to the police station, sir," the officer interrupted. "We'll take your statement there." He turned Rick toward the exit.

Ginny stood in the open doorway, her eyes fixed on the officer's hand clamped around Rick's arm as though he was the criminal, her expression stricken.

Rick tugged his arm free and reached for her hand. "This isn't what you think."

TEN

Could she have been any more gullible?

Ginny couldn't decide which felt worse, seeing Rick led out of church by a police officer, or hearing his words—*Ginny and I aren't a couple*. Obviously, she'd read too much into the achingly tender brush of his thumb across her lips last night.

To think she'd turned down her mechanic's perfectly respectable dinner invitation in the misguided hope Rick might make a better offer. What had she been thinking?

Eddie had lived in this town all his life. Made a decent living at the garage he'd taken over from his dad. She'd even gone to school with his sisters. His life was an open book, just what she wanted in a man.

"Come on," Kim said with just the right amount of commiseration. "Your uncle's driving Lori home. I'll take you to lunch."

In the parking lot, clusters of people talked at a feverish pitch. From the glances directed her way, the rumor mill hadn't failed to connect her to Rick. *Thank you, Lori.*

Except Ginny had been as thrilled as her sister to see Rick here.

Lord, please be with him. I wanted to believe Rick had escaped his past and we could find a way back to what we once had. Help it not hurt so much.

Kim steered her toward Ginny's car. "You're not going to believe what happened."

"I think I have a pretty good idea." Ginny disentangled herself from Kim's grasp and straightened the sleeves on her new outfit.

"You are so wrong, Ginny." Kim climbed into the passenger side and waited for Ginny to start the car. "Let's eat at Claire's Cuisine."

Ginny headed for the highway, scanning the mirrors for any sign of a tail. With Rick on his way to the police station, she could forget about him protecting her. And without any real idea of who had followed her last night, or why, the police weren't likely to take her fears seriously. "Well? Are you going to tell me what happened?"

"Mr. Robins tried to snatch Amy."

"Mr. Robins? Then why did—?"

Kim's smile could've lit a city block. "Duke stopped him!"

Ginny skidded the car onto the highway. "What do you mean stopped him?"

"You should've seen him. He pinned Robins in two seconds flat. If Duke ever wanted to give up construction, he'd make an amazing cop. He's got great instincts."

Ginny blinked at her friend. "Cop? Never."

From the flush of Kim's cheeks and the admiration in her voice, Ginny wondered if Kim wasn't a bit in love with *Duke*. She'd always been a police groupie.

Too bad Rick's prowess came from working the other side of the law. "Have you forgotten where he got those instincts?"

"Hey, I thought you decided to give the poor guy another chance. He came to church, didn't he?"

"Sure. He sat in the back row. I wouldn't have known he was there if Lori hadn't made a spectacle of pointing him out."

"Oh."

"Yeah, *oh*." Ginny pulled into the parking lot of Claire's Cuisine. "And let's not forget his Ginny-and-I-aren't-a-couple speech."

"You heard that, huh?"

"You know I did. Now can we please stop talking about him?"

"Don't you want to hear the rest of my story?"

Every last detail. Except the fact Rick was the hero of the story injected a little more sting into his rejection. Now she couldn't console herself with some fairy tale about his chivalrous desire to protect her from being associated with a criminal.

The restaurant, situated across the street from the police detachment, was crowded with the usual mix of folks in their Sunday best and cops in uniform. One guess which group Kim hoped to lollygag around. "Looks like we'll have to wait for a table. Why don't we go to—"

"Look, there he is." Kim pointed to a table where a surfer-looking type sat with…

Rick.

"You set me up."

"I did not. It was a lucky guess." She smirked. "A guy's gotta eat somewhere. Right?" Ginny turned to leave, but Kim grabbed her arm. "Oh, come on." Kim dragged Ginny toward him. "You can't let that gorgeous new dress go to waste."

Rick wore a tweed sports jacket that tugged at his broad shoulders and filled her with an irrational yearning to believe he was as upstanding as he looked.

Lord, what's wrong with me? The man has done nothing but feed me lines. Why can't I just forget him?

"We meet again," Kim said, stopping at their booth.

Rick jerked something off the table and shoved it into his pocket.

Ginny caught only a glimpse, but it'd looked like one of Uncle Emile's Harbor Creek sales pamphlets in a plastic bag.

"Won't you join us?" Rick said with an enthusiasm she might've mistaken for interest, if his gaze hadn't drifted toward the door as though he wanted to make a run for it.

So much for knocking his socks off with the new dress.

Rick motioned to the guy beside him. "This is my friend Zach."

"The Zach I talked to on the phone?" Kim tugged

Ginny down beside her on the bench opposite the pair. "Zach's a cop." Kim waggled her eyebrows, for Ginny's eyes only, then returned her attention to Rick's friend. "How do you two know each other?"

"We used to work together."

"In security," Rick added.

"Oh, so that's where you learned the takedown routine." Kim flashed Ginny a meaningful look she didn't want to begin to decipher.

For all she knew Zach was Rick's parole officer. Why else would an ex–gang member have a cop's number on speed dial?

And from the way he hid behind his menu, that hadn't been the only thing he'd neglected to tell her. No more secrets. *Right.* The guy had more secrets than the CIA.

"You should join the police force, Duke." Kim tapped his menu with her finger. "You'd be a natural. Wouldn't he, Zach? I don't know what we would've done if he hadn't shown up." Kim sucked in a breath without missing a beat. "Did they throw Robins in jail?"

"He's been charged with violating his restraining order, attempted kidnapping and uttering threats," Zach said.

Kim propped her elbows on the table and looked at him like a puppy drooling over a treat. "What made you become a cop?"

Ginny couldn't understand why her friend would want to date a guy who risked his life every day on the streets. Sure, being in law enforcement was a noble profession, but did Kim really want to marry a guy who faced the dregs of society on a daily basis?

Nightmares had plagued Ginny's soldier dad from his first tour of duty. She could still remember waking to his screams in the middle of the night.

The waitress took their orders, and Kim switched to probing Rick. "What about you, Duke? Did you ever think about becoming a cop?"

"Sure. What kid hasn't?"

"No, I mean *really* think about it?"

When Rick didn't respond, Zach gave him a nudge. "Tell them your story."

"Yeah," Rick admitted begrudgingly. "There was one time. I was leafing through comic books at a corner store when this guy in a ski mask came in waving a gun and demanded money. The lady behind the counter froze. I'd never seen that kind of fear on anyone's face before. Even her lips turned white. I wanted to save her so bad, but I was just a kid.

"A guy who'd been squatting to grab something from a bottom shelf motioned for me to get down. Then he ambushed the robber. It turned out my hero was an off-duty police officer." Rick's voice hitched. "I decided then and there I wanted to be just like that man when I grew up."

Moved by the regret that seemed to have Rick by the throat, Ginny said, "Well, I'm glad you changed your mind. I don't think I could date a cop."

Oops. Did she really just say that? Aloud?

Apparently, because Rick turned as sickly green as Lori's Gloworm. And wasn't that encouraging?

Zach wagged his finger from Ginny to Rick. "You two are dating?"

Ginny slipped low in her seat and let Kim field the question. Maybe she should be thankful that the idea of dating her made Rick look sick, because the old Rick would've quipped, "Not for lack of trying," and then watched with a wicked smile as her cheeks flamed.

Not *Duke*. He couldn't even scrounge up enough enthusiasm to tease. So she should just get over the silly dreams she'd let run amok in her head the past few days.

Rick touched her hand. "You okay?"

She nodded, but the sudden concern in his voice did funny things to her stomach.

"Why wouldn't you date a cop?" he asked, his voice low, almost sad.

"I could never marry someone with such a dangerous job. My dad was in the military and he died overseas and I could never put my children through what I went through." She fussed with her napkin. "No child should have to watch their daddy come home from work in a box."

Rick's heart lurched at her words, at the raw pain behind them, at the future they doomed.

He cupped his hand over hers and thrashed past the twisted mass of bitterness and sympathy wadded in his throat. "I'm so sorry."

Remembering the day his own dad died after he was run off the road, Rick stared at the shredded napkin clutched in Ginny's hand. If only he'd known his promise that day to continue being a cop would cost a piece of his soul…

Their food arrived and the conversation lapsed.

How could he deliberately lead Ginny on when she wouldn't want him—a cop—in her life once she knew the truth?

But given the incriminating note Zach dug out of Laud's garbage, what choice did he have?

Laud would sacrifice his niece in a heartbeat to save his own skin. Zach might've concluded Ginny was on the take with her uncle, but lowlifes like Laud survived by implicating innocents. No, Rick would sooner hand in his badge than hand over this case to someone else. To someone who didn't know Ginny like he did. If he stayed the course and proved to his meddling partner he hadn't lost his objectivity, he'd nail Laud and protect Ginny. He just prayed that when everything ended, she'd forgive him.

Kim fluttered her hands. "Hey, are the two of you coming to the fundraiser Ginny's organizing?"

"A fundraiser, huh?" The change in Zach's posture signaled his intention to take control of the conversation. "What other kind of work do you do for your uncle, Ginny?"

Rick pressed the toe of his shoe against Zach's shin, warning him to back off.

Ginny wiped her mouth with her napkin, and pitched a well-rehearsed explanation of the need for a community-based group home and the funds to operate it. Her enthusiasm was so contagious Rick almost whipped out his wallet and handed over all his cash.

Not Zach, who was no doubt thinking about the words *cut Ginny's take by five percent* scrawled on the brochure he'd recovered from Laud's garbage. Zach's expression hardened, turned all bad cop. "How much of a cut do you get?"

"Nothing." Ginny's voice shot up.

Rick ground his heel into his buddy's foot and Zach's nostrils flared. He should be happy Rick didn't kick him. How was he supposed to win Ginny's trust with his "friend" grilling her like a criminal?

"I'm doing this for my sister, not my own personal gain."

"So your uncle pays you nothing?"

"That's right."

Zach flicked Rick a glance that said *I rest my case.*

Rick planted his feet on the floor. They both knew her uncle wrote her a check every month. If Rick didn't know Ginny as well as he did, between the checks and the scrawl on the brochure, he might believe she was on the take, too.

Kim fidgeted, clearly uncomfortable with the simmering undercurrents. "Ginny writes web copy for a living."

"Oh, yeah?" Zach injected enough friendly interest into the question to not sound like a police interrogator. "Like those miracle diet letters that come in the mail?"

Ginny visibly cringed at the comparison. "Sort of."

Rick gave her a sympathetic look. While she couldn't deny that ads for fad diets and get-rich-quick schemes were a copywriter's bread and butter, he knew she refused to write for the scam artists.

"So how does that work?" Zach said.

"I'm paid royalties based on response rates."

"How do you know if the company reports the rates accurately?"

Clearly puzzled, Ginny frowned. "I guess I don't."

Of course! Ginny wrote sales brochures for her uncle. That explained the checks. And he likely sliced and diced her commission whenever it suited him. Rick touched two fingers to his temple in a subtle salute.

Zach answered with an almost imperceptible nod and touché glint in his eye.

Kim pulled a stack of purple stubs from her purse and waved them in the air. "Hey, we were talking about the fundraising gala. Remember? I happen to have tickets on me, if you'd like to come."

Kim's distraction pulled Zach's attention from Ginny.

She caught Rick's eye and tilted her head toward the pair.

Relishing the momentary connection, Rick set aside his own irritation with Zach to share a fleeting smile with Ginny over his buddy's obvious interest in her friend.

An ache rippled through Rick's heart. Ginny wasn't interested in dating a cop. Ever.

As Zach and Kim made plans to attend the gala

together, Rick's we're-not-a-couple comment hung in the silence between him and Ginny like the proverbial elephant in the room. "Ginny," he whispered, "about what I said at church."

"You don't owe me an explanation."

"You've got to understand that it's still not a good idea for us to be seen together—" he glanced at the crowd of diners "—socially."

"Of course." Ginny snapped open her purse and pulled out her wallet.

Rick stayed her hand, the warmth of her skin making his voice turn thick. "I'll take care of the bill."

She started to argue, but when she met his gaze, her words faltered. "Thank you," she said, then tugged on Kim's sleeve and practically sprinted for the exit.

Rick shoved aside his half-eaten lunch, tossed a pair of twenties on the table and took off after her. No matter how she felt about cops, or him, he needed to convince her he still cared for her before she told her uncle otherwise. Rick skirted tables and caught the door in her wake.

Grady, in jeans and a T-shirt that still stank of refuse, bumped Rick's shoulder. "Hey, just the man I need to talk to."

"Not now." Rick blew past the detective and into the parking lot. "Ginny, wait."

"I get it, okay." She strode toward her car as if she wore running shoes instead of two-inch heels. Heels that made her sleek legs look amazing.

Rick scouted the area with a sweeping glance then chewed the distance between them.

Kim—apparently, his only ally in this gig—took her sweet time getting to the car and jerked her head toward Ginny with a get-over-here glare that put the police captain's to shame.

Rick tapped on Ginny's window and she obliged him by rolling the glass down four inches.

"Call me paranoid," he said, hunkering to eye level, "but the last time you tore out of a restaurant parking lot, your brakes failed. I'd feel a whole lot better if you'd let me check over your car."

Fear flashed through her eyes, quickly replaced by a do-I-look-like-I-was-born-yesterday scowl. "You just finished telling me we shouldn't be seen together."

"Please," he said, letting his voice dip to the deep protective tone she always seemed to tug out of him.

"Oh, what's the harm?" Kim prodded. "Look at his face. The poor guy's worried about you."

She sighed, climbed out and then stood back, arms crossed over her chest, toe tapping, while Rick popped the hood and checked the belts and fluid levels.

Tap away, sweetheart. He'd rather have her irritated with him than roadkill.

Next, he shimmied under the car and checked the gas and brake lines.

"Satisfied?" she snapped when he wiggled back out, but her tone sounded far more irritated than she looked. Her expression had changed from annoyed to curious to almost appreciative.

He pulled a tissue from his pocket and wiped the grease from his hands. "Yup. Drive carefully. I'll be in touch."

She climbed into the car with a loud harrumph.

Yup, she knew he cared.

Zach caught Rick's shoulder. "What? You're not going to follow her?"

"Har, har. Now that you've had your laugh you can drive me back to the church to get my truck."

"Aren't you curious about what Grady found out?"

"I'm sure you'll tell me. Right after you explain what you thought you were doing grilling Ginny. 'Cause last time I checked—" Rick strode to Zach's pickup "—I was still in charge of this case."

"You saw the twinge of deceit in her face when she claimed her uncle paid her nothing. I know you noticed."

"She meant he paid her nothing for fundraising. Of course he pays her for writing sales brochures. He's probably cheating her, too. And she's too trusting to know it. No way has Ginny scored a piece of the action. Her mom's car is ancient, so was her own car, and their cupboard is stuffed with unpaid bills."

"Sounds like strong motivation to do whatever it takes to earn a piece of the pie."

"What pie?" If Rick weren't halfway sure Zach was just playing the devil's advocate, he'd sock him in the mouth for suggesting such a thing. And, okay, maybe he was letting his personal feelings get in the way of this case, but come on… "Laud's in debt up to his eyeballs. Trust me. I know Ginny. She's not knowingly doing anything illegal."

"You might be right. One of the prints Grady lifted off the brochure matched the thumbprint the local police pulled off your rock thrower's note."

"Finally we're getting somewhere. Okay, we'll need a female undercover officer. Try to get Terri. Have her schedule a meeting with Laud's salesman." Rick pulled out the brochure and looked at the photo on the attached business card. The weasel with the slicked-back hair had the same scrawny build as their hooded rock thrower. "We need this guy's prints. Terri can pose as a business owner interested in leasing an office suite. Did Grady learn anything off the street?"

"Yeah, a Russian named Petroski fronts money to businessmen. The loans are aboveboard, but well beyond the means of the client. When they can't pay, Petroski offers *alternative* financing options. Word on the street is, Laud refused to play the game. Go figure. The guy will burn buildings for the insurance, but won't launder money for the mob."

"So Petroski pressures Laud to pay up by threatening his family."

"We have nothing to connect Petroski to the attacks on Ginny or the break-in at your house."

"Yeah, we do. Our salesman Mr. Jones used to work for Petroski's realty company."

"How'd you find that out?"

"I saw Jones exiting Laud's office the day after the Harbor Creek fire and dug a little deeper into his history."

"Okay, so I think we can safely say you don't have an ex-con targeting you."

That was the best news Rick had heard in a week. Maybe he could take Ginny to the gala after all. "Except, how'd Jones connect my identities?"

"You told Laud that you used to go by Rick Gray."

"So you're saying Jones is playing both sides of the fence. Investigate me at Laud's request and target Ginny at Petroski's. But then why would Laud ask me to protect Ginny after Jones found the photo of me and Tom?"

"Maybe Jones didn't give Laud the photo."

Rick tensed. "Why?"

"That's what we need to find out."

ELEVEN

Monday morning Ginny stuffed sandwiches into Lori's lunch bag with only one thing on her mind. Work. Forget Rick. Forget the group home. Forget the upcoming gala. Between the twice weekly trips with Mom to the cancer clinic and the time spent soliciting donations for the fundraiser, Ginny had scarcely spent more than a few hours a day at her computer. No wonder Rick's cop friend had all but insinuated she skimmed the funds she raised to pay her bills.

She snorted. One look in her cupboard would put that accusation to rest.

But Kim had offered to drive Lori to her job at the chocolate factory and Mom to the hospital, so for today, Ginny could concentrate on catching up on the work that paid her bills. She loaded the last of the breakfast dishes into the dishwasher and gave a final swipe to the counter when the doorbell rang.

"Mom, Lori," Ginny called down the hall where her mother was coaxing Lori into her shoes. "Kim's here."

She threw the dead bolt and opened the door.

A delivery man stood where Kim should be. Ginny frantically clicked the lock on the screen door between them.

"Are you Miss Bryson?" the man asked.

"Yes." She memorized his features. Square face, gray hair swept over a bald spot, average build. Her gaze dropped to the long, narrow box in his hands. A flower box.

He rattled the handle of the screen door.

She glanced at the florist truck in the driveway and the neighbor walking by with his dog and figured she was safe. The moment she flipped the latch, the man opened the door and laid the box in her arms. "Have a nice day."

Her heart battered her ribs as she quickly shut and locked the door. Who would send her flowers?

Half-afraid they were from Eddie and more afraid they were from Rick, Ginny hid the box in the hall closet. They weren't from Rick. He wouldn't even be seen in public with her. How were they supposed to work together with Rick always avoiding her?

She dragged her thoughts away from Rick, who was *not* her priority today.

Mom ushered Lori, dressed with matching shoes, to the front door. Lori threw her arms around Ginny. "Bye, Gin."

Ginny squeezed her eyes closed and hugged her sister back, absorbing the unconditional love. Just two seconds ago she'd been impatient for Lori to leave so she could get to her computer. But Lori's hug reminded her why she'd put so much time and effort into the fundraiser.

Kim's car pulled to the curb and Lori trooped out the door, Mom silently trailing.

After waving them off, Ginny dug into the closet and stared at the box. It could be from the saboteur. Maybe even a bomb.

Sweat slicked her palms as she debated phoning Rick. If the flowers turned out to be from Eddie, she'd feel foolish.

With trembling fingers, she pried open the attached envelope. Tiny pink hearts decorated the card and Ginny's own heart burst into an erratic happy dance. Rick wanted to go with her to the gala. He'd even signed the card from Rick, not Duke.

Uncertainty swept over her and she cringed at how easily her feelings for him yo-yoed. Just yesterday at church, she'd automatically assumed the worst when that cop took him by the arm. And a few moments ago, she'd been certain he wouldn't send her flowers. She set the box on the kitchen table. Inside, a dozen long-stemmed roses lay nestled in a bed of fern. She lifted one to her cheek and its velvety softness felt like a tender kiss.

Good grief. She glanced at the digital clock on the microwave. She didn't have time for this. Dynovitamins wanted a new series of information pages to promote their products and the deadline loomed.

She arranged the flowers in a vase and carried it to her basement office. At her desk, she typed the client's web address into her computer and perused their site. The first step with every new client was always to figure out who she was dealing with. If she'd put the same effort into deciphering Rick, maybe she wouldn't be in this quandary over her feelings about him now.

She pulled up the analytics metrics and focused on the numbers. Low. No wonder the company wanted a website overhaul. Too many businesses made the mistake of posting pages that boasted about their company when they needed to make their message about their prospects' interests, needs and desires.

Ginny's gaze strayed to the vase of roses. Yellow. Her favorite color.

Oh, Rick knew all about how to meet his prospect's desires.

And there she went again—thinking about him.

She carried the flowers up to the living room. Out of sight. Out of mind. A stray checker bit into the bottom of Ginny's foot.

Lord, what am I supposed to do? I wish I could be like Lori and run to Rick with arms opened wide, freely forgiving, trusting that he's changed. But what if he hasn't?

Ignoring the tick of the mantel clock, Ginny reached for her Bible—another thing she'd neglected lately. She turned to her favorite verse. "If you call out for insight and cry aloud for understanding and if you look for it as for silver and search for it as for hidden treasure, then you will understand the fear of the Lord and find the knowledge of God. For the Lord gives wisdom."

Wisdom. The word leaped out at her. Wisdom was exactly what she needed, that and assurance that her feelings weren't deceiving her, that letting Rick back into her life, back into Lori and Mom's lives, wasn't a mistake.

Please, Lord, show me what to do.

Trust. The word whispered through her mind. Yes, God would guide her in His time.

In the meantime, she had a job to finish. She dove into the project and became so absorbed with her writing that her conscience scarcely pricked when she ignored the doorbell.

Then a shadow crept over her desk.

Glancing up, she glimpsed a dark figure. With her gaze pinned to the window and her heart hammering her ribs, she groped for the cordless phone.

The doorbell trilled a second time.

And whoever was at the door *knew* she was home.

Phone in hand, her thumb on the last one of 9-1-1, she ran up the stairs and nudged aside the front curtain. At the sight of Eddie, the breath rushed from Ginny's chest. Irritation immediately overrode her relief.

She yanked open the door. "What are you doing here?" she said as sweetly as she could manage, considering he'd been slinking around her house. She had work to do and precious few hours left before Mom and Lori returned.

He held up a handful of unopened mail. "I found these in your glove compartment and thought I'd save you a trip to the garage to pick them up."

"Thank you," she said without stepping back, a move he might misinterpret as an invitation to come in.

"Happy to help. Anytime. Um." Eddie toed the threshold with his work boot. "I was wondering if you'd come to the fundraising gala with me."

Thankful Rick's timely invitation spared her from hurting Eddie's feelings by turning him down outright, she said, "I'm sorry, someone else has already asked me."

"I see. Okay, then, I'll, um…get going."

Ginny locked the door behind him, and thumbed through the stack of envelopes as she returned to her office. A statement from Uncle Emile caught her attention. She glanced at the time and ripped open the envelope.

Her heart sank. For the third month in a row, the amount was low. Too low. She pulled up her accounting files, verified the numbers, did some calculations. The amount was definitely too low. And after the disturbing scenario Zach painted yesterday, she suspected Uncle Emile's accountant was doing some creative bookkeeping at her expense.

Knowing she wouldn't be able to concentrate until she dealt with the problem, she scrounged up the courage to call Uncle Emile.

"Ginny," he said in his I-know-you-don't-understand-business voice. "The economy's flat right now. Everyone's profits have shrunk."

"No, I ran the numbers. The statement isn't accurate. I'm sure he's bilking us. We need an audit."

"Now, now, calm down. I will iron this out," he promised. "No reason for you to worry. You're busy enough with grant applications and next week's gala." He paused. "What you need is a break. Meet me at the group home in half an hour. I still owe you a tour."

"I can't today. I have a lot of writing left to do."

"Nonsense, a break will do you good."

From unhappy experience, Ginny knew arguing with Uncle Emile once he'd made up his mind was utterly pointless. Better to go to the work site for fifteen minutes, question him about the numbers and then come straight back to finish the website before Lori and Mom got home.

Too much time later Ginny swerved to miss a jumble of aluminum scraps and parked beside Uncle Emile's BMW. Mangled slabs of insulation and scraps of lumber littered the construction site, not unlike the emotional mess the men in her life had wrought.

At Rick's request, the cops had beefed up patrols in her neighborhood. And as she climbed into her car, Zach happened to be cruising by. He'd inspected her car, and then urged her to be cautious. She glanced at the console clock. Constantly checking her mirrors had added an extra five minutes to her trip, on top of the ten minutes Zach had burned. At this rate, she'd be lucky to get home before Mom. Let alone finish the website.

Rick grinned at her from the front door of the two-story colonial and her stomach twirled. He'd want an answer about the gala and she still hadn't made up her mind.

Dressed in faded jeans and a white T-shirt, he looked like an honest-working Joe—a ruggedly handsome, calendar-quality, working Joe. Any girl would be thrilled to attend the gala on his arm.

Uncle Emile greeted her with a kiss and she showed him the statements she'd brought.

"See. These are the figures that prove—"

Rick sauntered toward them, his gaze flicking from their faces to the documents.

"We'll discuss this another time," Uncle Emile said, giving the first page a cursory glance before tossing the stack into his car. "Duke! My niece has been so busy courting rich businessmen for donations that she hasn't had a tour."

After one last glance at the documents, a mischievous twinkle lit Rick's eye. "Hmm, I might be persuaded to make a donation if it comes with *courting*."

Caught off guard by his flirting, Ginny shyly whispered, "Thank you for the flowers."

He took her hand and threaded his fingers through hers. "And."

He smelled of coffee and sawdust and an intriguing mixture of suntan lotion and pine. She leaned closer to savor it, and the pounding in her chest eclipsed the sound of hammers and saws. "And?"

"And will you go to the gala with me?"

Laud cleared his throat with an I'm-still-here cough. "Well, my dear, it looks like I can leave you in Duke's capable hands."

"What? No, you can't go yet. We need to discuss… uh…" She swallowed, not wanting to give Rick another reason to mistrust her uncle's colleagues. Not until she had all the facts. She glanced at her watch—seven more minutes gone. "Um, we need to discuss that other matter before you leave."

"I'll deal with it. Don't worry."

She sunk her teeth into her bottom lip. What a waste of time this'd turned into.

The gentle squeeze of Rick's hand drew her thoughts back to him, and her heart did a tiny flip. She might as well salvage the trip by talking to Rick about his surprising invitation to the gala. She'd told Eddie she had a date, but maybe that had been a mistake.

"I'll take good care of her," Rick heard himself saying, and wondered if he'd laid on the interest a little too thick to inspire Laud's continued trust. Clearly, from the way Ginny had shied away from discussing her business in front of him, Rick hadn't won *her* trust yet. A situation he planned to remedy. His gut told him the papers she'd brought Laud were connected to the info Zach uncovered yesterday. Info that might implicate Ginny if it were misinterpreted.

He led her inside. "Anything I can do to help?"

"No, no. It's just an accounting glitch. Nothing to do with the group home."

Not wanting to appear too curious about why she was challenging Laud's accounting, Rick dipped his head sideways until she met his gaze. "I'm still happy to help any way I can. Okay?"

Her responding smile did dangerous things to his heart. Steering her away from the crew hanging drywall, he whispered close to her ear, "You never answered my other question."

"Other question?"

"My invitation."

"Oh, *that* question," she said, teasing in her voice.

The sunshine splashing through the windows turned her hair to gold, and Rick's mind reeled back to the time they'd hiked the Niagara Escarpment. The striking contrast of the autumn colors to the deep blue sky had been spectacular. The kind of scenery that gave a guy ideas. And drawn in by that same radiant smile, he hadn't been able to stop himself from gathering her in his arms. She'd tasted of goodness and patience and happily ever afters.

He closed his eyes against the hopelessness that piggybacked that thought.

"Well, I don't know," she continued in her teasing voice. "You'd have to be *seen* with me. In—*gasp*—public!"

He chuckled. "I'm willing to take my chances, if you are."

"Hmm, that depends on why you're asking. To be with *me*? Or to be my bodyguard?"

"Definitely to be with you. Being your bodyguard is purely a fringe benefit."

"Then I accept."

Her sweet laugh zinged through his chest. He

opened his arms for a celebratory hug, only to be thwarted by two guys jockeying past with a sheet of drywall.

Ginny glanced at her watch. "Yikes, I need to go. I have a ton of work to finish before Mom and Lori get home."

"Not a chance." He waited for the guys to pass and then caught her hand. "I haven't shown you Lori's room yet." *Or found out what you're hiding.* He led her to the suite in the southeast corner. "It has a fantastic view of the bay."

"Wow. Lori can spy on the neighborhood from here." Ginny pointed east. "Look. Isn't that Uncle Emile's car parked on the next street over?"

Rick glanced in the direction Ginny pointed. Storm clouds had gathered over the lake and the dark water was as choppy as his insides. He couldn't discern one car from another. Maybe he needed his eyes checked. He'd missed too much lately. But he hadn't missed Ginny's deflated expression when her uncle tossed aside her papers. "That accounting glitch you wanted to talk to him about must've been pretty important to drag you away from your work." Guilt needled Rick as Ginny, clearly flustered by his question, wandered through the rooms. "You seemed pretty upset when Laud sloughed it off."

"That's because I really do need to get back to work." She headed for the stairs.

"Hey, wait up. You never told me what you think of the place."

She turned to him, tears shimmering in her eyes. "It's beautiful."

"Then why the tears?" he whispered, reaching out to her.

"I hadn't expected letting go to be so…hard. With my workload lately, I'd looked forward to being relieved of the responsibility for Lori's care. But she's my sister."

"And she knows you love her." His heart crunched in his chest. He'd been so focused on what was up with Laud's accounting that he hadn't recognized what kind of mixed feelings this place roused in Ginny. "There's no easy answer. You have to trust God to lead you to what's best. Everything will work out. You'll see."

She wiped her eyes. "You're right. And I really do need to go now."

He followed her down the stairs. "Ginny, I don't want to pry where it's none of my business, but about this accounting glitch. Could it be connected to our rock thrower or your brake failure?"

Her grimace said she'd considered the possibility. "I know we said no secrets, but I wanted to give Uncle Emile a chance to look into the problem first, because I knew you'd blame him as soon as I told you."

"Told me what?"

Ginny cleared the stairs and reached for the door. "Let's give Uncle Emile until tomorrow. Then I'll tell you. Okay?" She stepped outside and her scream—cut short—pierced the air.

TWELVE

Rick hurdled the last four stairs and blew out the door of the group home at a run.

Ginny's body lay crumpled in the dirt.

His heart slammed into his ribs as he skidded to his knees. "Ginny, talk to me." He stroked the hair from her face, and she let out a weak groan. He scanned the dumbfounded faces of his crew. "Tell me what happened! Somebody—"

"Dunno… I was inside… I didn't see anything," the men on his crew all mumbled at once.

Ginny curled into a ball. "Something fell…"

A hunk of two-by-four lay on the ground and one of his men pointed to an open second-story window. "It must've fallen from up there."

Rick peered at the window and then his crew. "Where's Vic? Who else is missing?"

"Vic's out back," Mike spoke up. "Loading the truck for a dump run."

"Get him, then run upstairs. I want to know where everyone was when this happened."

Ginny cupped the side of her head. "I don't feel so good."

Her broken voice shredded Rick's insides. He needed to figure out who did this to her, but first he had to take care of her. He cradled her neck in his hands. "How's your vision? Are you dizzy?"

"A little," she admitted.

He helped her stand. "I'll drive you to the doctor."

"No, that's not—" She swayed and he gathered her into his arms.

"If it's all the same to you, I'd like a second opinion."

She curled into his chest without another word of protest, and the sight of her trust—when all he'd cared about was grilling her for information—took his breath away.

Vic strutted around the corner carrying an armload of aluminum scraps. "You wanted to see me?"

"Where were you five minutes ago?"

Vic took one look at Ginny and jutted his thumb toward the back of the building. His armload clattered to the dirt. "Cleaning up." His expression went blank, his tone neutral—the practiced defense of a criminal used to warding off accusations.

Mike ran out of the building. "No one's up there, boss."

Vic looked from Mike to Rick. "You looking for the kid in the hooded sweatshirt?"

The question exploded in Rick's chest. *Jones.* It had to be. The realization deep-sixed any hope the incident was an accident.

"You want us to run out there and find the kid?" one of his burlier workers asked, making a show of punching his fists into his palms.

Rich shoved his feelings into a hard ball to deal with later. "Yeah," he said, certain Laud's salesman would be long gone. "If you find the guy, hang on to him and call me on my cell. I'm taking Ginny to the clinic."

He had to warn her that someone was targeting her so she'd be on her guard. Never mind that he might be the one endangering her. He'd just blown any notion of fooling her stalker into believing he didn't care for her.

An hour and a half later, Rick carried her into her home and laid her on the sofa. The fragrance of roses brought a smile to his lips. "Now, stay put. I'll get you ice for that goose egg."

She wriggled herself up, wincing. "I don't have time to lie down. I have to work."

He eased her back down. "The doctor said you need to rest."

"I'll rest later, once Lori's home."

"You can't shrug off a concussion. If you don't rest now, you'll pay for it. Trust me, I know." He tucked an afghan under her chin and slipped into the kitchen to try Zach's number again. He'd gotten nothing but the answering machine while Ginny was with the doctor, and this was not a conversation Rick wanted Ginny to overhear. If he was going to keep her safe, he needed a location on Jones, and fast.

Somehow they had to bring him in without exposing the operation.

Rick's thumb froze over the buttons. Jones was in a meeting with Terri this afternoon. He couldn't have been their hooded runner.

Did Vic make up the generic description to throw the heat off himself?

Maybe there wasn't a runner at all. Laud's car was parked on the next street. What if Ginny stumbled on to something bigger than the skimmed royalty checks she'd told him about on the way to the doctor? Something Laud couldn't afford to become known?

No one would think twice about seeing him onsite. Rick scrolled through his messages. Laud still hadn't responded to Rick's six attempts to reach him on his cell phone.

He tried the office again. But Mary didn't pick up, either. What was this? National Don't-Answer-Your-Phone Day?

He didn't dare leave Ginny alone. She'd likely fall down the stairs trying to get to her computer. Proof sounded from the next room.

Rick grabbed an icepack and hurried to where Ginny clung to the edge of the sofa. As he coaxed her into lying back down, the reality of how close she'd come to being more seriously injured, maybe killed, squeezed his chest. "Ginny, please, you have to rest. I don't know what I would've done if—"

She touched his lips. "I'm okay."

"You're not. You need to rest. Seeing you hurt was like reliving my parents' accident. I can't lose you, too." The words poured out of Rick's mouth before he had a chance to censor them.

"You've never talked about your parents. What happened?"

A true professional would tell her that they died in a car accident, end of story. For a second, Rick considered doing just that, but the tender concern in her eyes made him want to give her more. That, and the realization that for the first time today she wasn't angling to get to her computer.

He dragged in a breath. "A black SUV rammed the side of my parents' vehicle and forced them off the road."

At Ginny's gasp, Rick closed his eyes.

He could still visualize every second of that night. The moon rising above the trees—huge and sickly yellow. The sound of the tires when they skidded into the gravel. The surreal effect of the swirling lights on the leaves.

"By the time I got to them, fire trucks, police cars, ambulances lined the road. But Dad's car lay flipped over in the ditch with a guardrail knifed through its hood."

How many times had he been called to an accident site and marveled at the improbability of a chain of events? How cars hit the guardrail at exactly the wrong angle so instead of a paint scrape, the impact sent it, and the people inside, flying. But bad luck had nothing to do with this accident.

Even now, the roar of the power saw ratcheted through his body. The gasoline fumes coiled in his stomach. "My dad got pinned by the steering column, and while firefighters fought to peel back the door, internal injuries stole his life."

It's over, Mom had chanted deliriously. But Dad had fixed his eyes on Rick and with his dying breath said, *It's not over, son. You can't let the criminals win. Promise me....*

Tears blurred Rick's eyes as he remembered how he'd clung to Dad's hand, felt the life slip away and vowed to continue his father's quest for justice.

Ginny squeezed his arm. "Why would someone do that to your parents?"

"My dad..." Rick fought the tightening in his throat. "My dad was scheduled to testify in a high-profile mafia case."

"Why didn't the police give him protection? They should have known someone might—"

"No." Rick shifted his gaze to the window. "My dad wouldn't have asked for protection." Then before he could stop himself, or maybe because he desperately needed Ginny to understand what was at stake, he said, "Because my dad was a cop."

Jumbled clues connected in Ginny's mind as Rick cradled his head in his palm. His takedown of Mr. Robins—great instincts, Kim had said. His barrage of questions about her accident. His story about the off-duty cop he'd wanted to emulate. How could she have missed his peculiar anguish when Kim gushed on and on that he should be a cop?

Ginny touched his arm. "That cop. The one you

idolized. The one who stopped the robbery. He was your dad?"

"Yes," Rick moaned, as if he'd had to claw the admission out of his throat.

"His death…is that why you changed your mind about becoming a cop?"

He lifted his gaze to hers. "Ginny, I—" He clenched his jaw. Glanced away. "My dad used to say that he couldn't quit because that would be letting the bad guys win."

"I'm so sorry." Is that why Rick had never wanted to talk about his family? Had he been too ashamed that he'd become like the men his father sent to jail every day? "Did the police catch the man who hit your parents' car?"

A hollowness crept into Rick's eyes. "Eventually, yes."

After the glimpse he'd given her into his deepest hurts, she longed to understand him better, but his revelation sucked him into a place far away.

"Waiting for justice is hard," she said finally. "I found that out when Lori was little and the neighborhood bully picked on her."

Rick stiffened in that protective way he had about him that always squeezed her heart.

"I vowed to teach him a lesson, but my Bible-thumping neighbor overheard me and quoted a Bible verse about waiting for the Lord's justice."

"'The Lord longs to be gracious to you; He rises

to show you compassion. For the Lord is a God of justice. Blessed are all who wait for Him.'"

"Yeah, that's the one," she said, letting her curiosity slip into her voice.

Rick had recited the verse without a moment's hesitation, but then frowned, as if the words made him uncomfortable. Which was odd, since he must've committed the Scripture to memory for a reason.

When he didn't offer an explanation, Ginny continued her story. "I wasn't a believer when I was young, so I wasn't sure I believed my neighbor. With my dad dead, and my mom...well... It hadn't felt like God was interested in showing my family much compassion."

The furrow in Rick's brow deepened. "What happened?"

Pretty sure he'd caught the slip about Mom, Ginny hesitated.

Rick touched her hand. "What's wrong?"

"Your construction crew is still hammering in my brain."

"I'm so sorry."

"It's not your fault." The accident itself had faded to the back of her mind, eclipsed by far sweeter experiences. The protective feel of Rick's arms. The heart-tugging concern in his gaze. And the sweetest of all, the sound of his quiet voice praying for her as he drove to the clinic.

"I was in the wrong place at the wrong time. Kind of like what happened to Lori's bully—only in his case, it was no accident. The next day, his dad *happened* to visit my neighbor and overheard the boy tease Lori." Ginny grinned. "After his father got through with him, the boy never bothered Lori again."

Rick didn't laugh as she'd expected. "Ginny, this wasn't an accident."

Her pulse quickened and the rush of blood intensified the throbbing in her head. "Of course it was an accident."

"Didn't you hear what Vic said? He saw a kid in a hooded sweatshirt running from the site."

Rick's bleak expression dried her mouth.

"Who else knew you were coming to the construction site today?"

"No one. When I called my uncle about the payment issue, he told me I needed a break and wouldn't take no for an answer."

"The tour was your uncle's idea?"

"Yes."

"Anyone see you leave?"

"Only Zach."

"Did you stop anywhere on the way?"

"No." She jerked up, and the pressure in her head skyrocketed.

"Ginny," Rick said, coaxing her to lie back. Then his voice grew more urgent. "I need you to concentrate. Did you notice a vehicle trailing you?"

Ginny pressed her palm to her aching head, knowing exactly which vehicle Rick meant. "No. And I kept a careful watch."

"I'm sorry to press you. I don't want to upset you."

"Upset me? You're downright scaring me."

Mom trundled into the room dressed in jeans and a blouse that looked like they'd been slept in. "I thought I heard voices."

Rick shot to his feet. "Sorry to disturb you. I didn't realize you were home." He tilted his head toward Ginny and gazed at her with...

Ginny blinked. Wow, those had to be some powerful pain meds the doctor slipped her, because if she didn't know better, she'd have sworn she saw love in Rick's soft eyes.

"I'm afraid Ginny was in an accident at the construction site."

"Oh dear, are you okay?" Rick moved aside and Mom knelt next to the sofa.

Ginny soaked in her concern. She couldn't remember the last time Mom had spoken to her with such compassion. The touch of her trembling fingers felt like a balm.

Ginny blinked back tears. "I have a brutal headache."

"She has a concussion and needs to take it easy for a few days," Rick added.

Like that was going to happen, when he'd filled her head with nightmares of some hit man after her.

Mom rose suddenly. "Where was Emile when this happened?"

Rick turned his face from Ginny's view, but she sensed a hesitation in his voice. "Why do you ask?"

Rick and Mom spoke in subdued tones, and Ginny

didn't have the energy to listen in, let alone get back to her computer or interrogate Rick. She closed her eyes, helpless against the pull of fatigue and pain.

Some time later, a cool hand touched her forehead. "Ginny." Rick's warm breath caressed her neck. "I need to look around the construction site, see if I can find out how this happened. I'll be back to check on you soon. Okay?" His voice turned strangely hoarse.

She lifted her lashes and met his gaze—a smoky gaze that soon slid to her lips as his hands gingerly glided through her hair, avoiding the bump and leaving a delicious tingle in their trail. He cradled her head, drawing her closer, and kissed her with mind-blowing tenderness.

The kiss lasted only a moment. A heart-stopping, glorious moment.

Then he left.

Rick peeled out of Ginny's driveway with Mrs. Bryson's words still ringing in his ears. How could he have missed that key bit of information for so long?

He was seriously losing it.

Rick took the corner without stopping and headed straight for Laud's office. Halfway there, he phoned Zach.

"What's up?"

"Laud's got a life insurance policy on Ginny and her mom."

Zach whistled. "So you think he's playing you?"

"I don't know. I'm going to see him now. If he

thinks—" Rick bit off the thought. "Meet me at the construction site in an hour."

"Are you sure you want to confront Laud when you're this upset?"

"He told me to protect her, didn't he?" Rick gunned past a slow-moving truck. "Well, he's about to get a taste of just how protective I can be."

"Whoa, back up. I can't believe a lousy insurance policy has you this riled."

"If you bothered to check your messages, you'd know that a two-by-four clobbered Ginny at the construction site today. She could've been killed."

"And you think Laud did it? Was he even there?"

"Yes, no. I don't know." Rick rammed his stick shift into third and stepped on the gas. "He left Ginny with me. Said he had a meeting. But she spotted his car on the next street over. He could've easily snuck back."

"Are you hearing yourself? Laud's too smart to do something that stupid. Don't let your emotions screw this up."

"Vic saw a guy in a hooded sweatshirt run in that direction."

"And you believe him?" Zach said incredulously.

"Someone threw that hunk of wood at Ginny," Rick shot back. "Jones was in a meeting with Terri at the time. And Ginny's on to Laud's book cooking."

"You think Laud would take out his own niece?" Zach's voice rose in disbelief.

"The man took out his own wife!"

"You don't know that," Zach said. "The fire marshal said she was smoking in bed."

"The fire started from a cigarette next to the bed. Not in it."

"Could've still been her own fault. And that was over twenty-five years ago. You've got to calm down, or you're going to blow your case. This could've been an accident, too, pure and simple."

"You're forgetting Ginny's brakes."

"She drives around construction sites. She might have hit a rock like the mechanic said."

"I can't believe you're saying this."

"Well, you'd better listen. Captain Drake thinks Ginny's new car was a payoff."

"A payoff? No way. Where'd Drake get an idea like that?"

"He ran into Mary at the courthouse."

Rick slapped his hand against the steering wheel and bit back a few choice words. "What else did Mary tell him?"

"You're missing the point. You never told Drake about Mary. He's spitting bullets. Face it. Your obsession with Ginny's safety has blinded you to the truth."

"Obsession?"

"Yes. You have a huge conflict of interest here. You never should've taken this case."

Rick twisted his hands around the steering wheel. "You don't have to tell me. Lying to Ginny is eating me alive."

The aching look she'd given him after he told her about his parents had made him want to tell her everything. And from the way she yielded to his kiss, he thought she just might forgive him for deceiving her. "I've never questioned what we have to do to bring down a criminal. I mean, I know God hates lying, but we're serving a greater purpose here, right?"

"That's between you and God."

Rick eased off the gas pedal. With the long hours he'd been putting in, it'd been weeks since he'd dug into God's Word, let alone shared some serious face time.

"God hates lying every bit as much as he hates murder. So if lying to Ginny about who you are and what you do is eating at you, maybe He's trying to tell you something."

"I can't quit." Rick swerved onto Laud's street without bothering to slow. "I promised Ginny I'd finish the home."

"Your job is to nail Laud, *not* to build that group home."

Five minutes later, Rick stormed into Laud's office without knocking.

Laud spun toward him, looking haggard. "Duke, what in the name of all that's holy are you doing? I told you to protect my niece." His hand shook as he poured himself a glass of water and popped an aspirin. "Is she all right?"

Rick jutted his chin toward the bottle. "Her headache's a lot worse than yours, but she'll live."

Laud snapped on the lid and pitched the bottle into his desk drawer. "I want whoever is responsible for this accident fired. Immediately."

"This wasn't an accident."

"What are you saying?"

Rick closed in on him. "I'm saying someone deliberately dropped that piece of wood out of a two-story building when Ginny walked within range."

The blood drained from Laud's face. But was his shock from failing to make the incident look like an accident or was it genuine torment over Ginny's injuries?

"Did you see who did it?"

Rick's gaze flicked to the murky gray sky outside the picture window. "No."

"I told you to get this guy." Laud slammed his fist onto the desk. "I will not tolerate him making my niece a pawn."

"If someone did this to pressure you to pay your debts, why hasn't he revealed himself so you'd get the message?"

"I got the message—loud and clear—but I don't have the money."

"You drive a BMW, wear thirty-five-hundred-dollar suits and you just bought your niece a nice-looking used car."

"In my business, appearance is everything." His gaze shifted to the window. "Unfortunately, my… shall we say, foreign business partners believe the appearances all too well and think I'm holding out on them."

"They who? Have they contacted you? Made threats?"

"They hurt my niece!"

Something about Laud's response felt a little too rehearsed. Was he deflecting the blame to hide his attempts on Ginny's life? Or was the Russian mafia really applying the pressure? Or was Laud completely paranoid, when Ginny's assailant actually wanted revenge on Rick?

Rick planted his hands on Laud's desk and leaned forward—up close and personal. "If you want me to stop them, I need more information."

"I've told you everything I know. It's Petroski. He needs to be stopped."

Why couldn't Rick have a voice recorder in his pocket when he needed one?

Recording Laud contracting a hit would be ten times better than contracting an arson. Rick leveled his gaze at Laud. "Are you asking me to kill this man?"

THIRTEEN

In the front hall, Lori tossed off her shoes with two jarring thuds. Ginny squished a pillow over her head.

"Your mom said Duke spent most of the afternoon here," Kim whispered, tugging the pillow aside.

Warmth flooded Ginny's cheeks. What was she supposed to make of Rick's kiss? She could still taste the coffee on his lips, feel the gentle pressure of his arms around her. She chewed on her bottom lip, but a smile worked its way out.

"Oooh. Do tell."

"I think he's appointed himself my guardian."

"Yummy."

Ginny swatted Kim's arm. "You're terrible."

"Hey, don't tell me it's not a little thrilling to have a man bent on protecting you. I see the dreamy look in your eye."

"Hello? He says someone tried to kill me."

"Do you believe him?"

"Uh, yeah!"

"Oh." Kim sobered, but only for a moment. "Look

on the bright side. It's not every day a girl has a knight in shining armor ride to her rescue."

Yeah, so what if his armor was a little tarnished? He'd bared his deepest hurts to her today. He wouldn't have done that if he didn't plan on sticking around. Would he? "I think I've figured out why Duke got messed up with that gang. His dad was a cop."

"Didn't I tell you he had good instincts?"

"He said his dad was killed by someone he was supposed to testify against."

"Oooh, so maybe Duke joined the gang to get the proof to nail his dad's murderer."

"It seems like something he'd do."

"So you're going to give him another chance?"

If Ginny could go by his tormented apologies, and soul-spilling revelation, not to mention his kiss, he certainly had feelings for her. And she couldn't deny her own.

"Yoo-hoo…earth to Ginny… Anybody home?"

"Okay, yes, if Duke asked me, I might consider dating him again."

Rick's rumbly voice drifted into the room a second before he appeared. "That's the best news I've heard all day."

Ginny sprang to a sitting position. Then immediately caught the back of the sofa and waited for the room to stop spinning.

Rick flipped on the overhead light, or maybe the twinkle in his eye had chased away the shadows.

Kim pulled a twenty-dollar bill out of her wallet and pressed it into Rick's hand. "Pizza's due any minute."

Rick turned his hand over, returning the money. "I'll take care of it. Thanks."

The tender look Rick gave Ginny after the door closed sent her heart twittering. Too bad she only had three seconds to enjoy the sensation before Lori barreled into the room.

"Duke here. Duke here."

Ginny would've smiled if not for the way her sister's shrill cry reverberated in her head. She lay back on the sofa and tried to focus. This was no time to let her emotions run amok. If she really was in danger, what were they supposed to do about it?

Rick caught Lori's hand. "Whoa there, Ginny needs to rest."

"Gin hurt. Head boo-boo."

"That's right." Rick coaxed Lori into a chair. "How about you look at your picture book?"

Lori shook her head with gale-force thrusts. "Checkers."

"Not tonight, sweetie. I need to talk to Ginny."

Lori jutted out her bottom lip. "Checkers."

"Lori, I said no. I need you to be good."

She crossed her arms. "Me good."

"Yes, you're a very good girl."

"Me good," she repeated, this time with sunshine in her voice.

Rick's conspiratorial wink in Ginny's direction unleashed a flurry in her middle. How was it that he could have such a calming effect on her sister yet whip her own emotions into a whirlwind?

He must've gone home and showered because as he shimmied close and cradled her hand between his, the scent of his soap and freshly laundered shirt made homey feelings curl in her chest.

"How are you feeling?"

"From the two-by-four? Or the psycho trying to kill me?" Her throat thickened. "What did you find out?"

"By the time I got to the construction site, it was spotless. We never clean up like that. I'm afraid someone on my crew didn't want any evidence found."

"Or they were afraid the labor board would be all over the place after the accident got reported."

"Maybe."

"So what do we do now?"

He stroked her hair with indescribable tenderness. "I want you to stay home until we can figure out who's behind these attacks."

"No way. I won't hide away like a timid mouse. And I certainly won't let some bully jeopardize the construction on Lori's home. If I ask Uncle—"

"Ginny…" The anguish in Rick's voice trembled through her. "I'm not sure your uncle can be trusted."

"How can you say that? He's the one who asked you to protect me."

"Yes, and I can't keep you safe if you gallivant around the countryside sticking your nose where it doesn't belong." He pulled a list from his pocket.

"But you can help. These are the names your uncle gave me. Do some research online and see what you can find out about them."

Recognizing her uncle's scrawl, Ginny took the paper. "What could these men possibly gain by hurting me?"

"Your uncle owes people money. Your accident was a threat to ensure he pays."

"That's crazy. He has gobs of money. He just bought me a car."

"Appearance means everything to your uncle. Remember? How can you be sure he hasn't gotten in over his head?"

Guilt swamped her. If what Rick said about Uncle Emile was true, by asking for a car she'd made his situation that much worse.

Rick stepped outside Mary's apartment building and glanced at his watch. He barely had time to catch Ginny before she left for the ballpark. After three days of being sequestered in her house without incident, and unconvinced by her online research that any of her uncle's associates were dirty, she'd refused to stay put a minute longer. Danger or no danger.

With a promise from Mary to stop meddling, and documents in hand, Rick hurried toward his truck. Sure, Mary was only trying to help, but she'd already made his life miserable by telling Captain Drake about Ginny's car. And Drake still fumed over Rick's failure to disclose Mary's association with Laud.

The man had stopped short of authorizing a hit, but

Rick had enough evidence to arrest him for fraud—not nearly severe enough punishment for what he'd done or was capable of doing. Seeing Tom's photograph on Mary's window ledge and thinking about the life insurance policy Laud had taken out on Ginny had steeled Rick's determination. Laud didn't deserve to see daylight for a long, long time.

Hope that after this case wrapped up Ginny might still want to seek refuge in his arms did dangerous things to Rick's heart. She'd made it unequivocally clear, more than once, that she couldn't love someone who lied. And he practically made a living out of it. But he'd moved past hoping she'd merely forgive him for keeping her in the dark about his job to dreaming she might want him to stay…forever.

Forget that she thought she could never marry a cop. When he'd heard her scream outside the group home, every protective instinct he possessed had sprung to life inside him. Since then, he'd resorted to praying God would change her opinion about cops, and that the truth of what he *was* wouldn't seem nearly as bad as the life she imagined he'd once led.

Rick scanned the area as he walked to his truck. The street, filled earlier with kids playing hockey, now lay deserted, but Rick couldn't shake the feeling of being watched.

A sudden sound drew him around.

Just a crumpled fast-food bag blowing across the street.

Shaking off the antsy feeling, he reached for the

truck's door handle. A fist blurred past his face, clipped his jaw.

His head jerked back and a second punch slammed into his ribs, the pain so sharp it swiped his breath.

"What are you doing sneaking around here?" his assailant hissed, fist pulled back ready to strike again.

Pulse roaring, Rick hunched over and spit out a mouthful of blood. "How'd you get out?"

"Good behavior." His lips curled into a sadistic smile. "And when I'm done with you, you'll curse the day you ever stuck your nose into my business."

FOURTEEN

Ginny helped the next batter get set up, then stepped away from the plate. On the sidelines, Kim snapped her phone shut and shook her head.

Why wasn't Rick answering his phone? He knew they had a game tonight. Ginny checked the streets around the park for the hundredth time. After the way he'd practically begged her not to leave the house, how could he stand them up?

Something had to be wrong. He wouldn't just not show.

Parents and siblings lined the stands shouting encouragement. Neighborhood children romped in the playground. No one paid Ginny any particular attention. But she dutifully scanned the parked cars and benches as Rick had instructed. His overprotectiveness was endearing, especially when he stopped by every night on the pretense of checking up on her and then stayed for hours to talk. While they hadn't shared another kiss, she was pretty sure she saw the desire to simmering in his eyes. Somehow his restraint, as though he didn't want to push, made her heart reach out all the more.

"Ginny."

She jumped at Kim's voice. The kids loped in, shedding their team bibs, and Ginny gave her head a shake. "What happened?"

"Game's over." Kim returned the cell phone. "Maybe Duke got caught up in work and lost track of time."

"That's not like him." Ginny clutched the discarded bibs to her chest. She didn't want to believe he'd stood them up, but she preferred that option to the other scenarios she'd imagined. "I'll drive by the construction site on my way home. If he's not there, I'm calling the hospital and—" Then what? She didn't even know where he lived.

"Take it easy. I called a friend in the E.R. Duke's not there."

"What if he got attacked and can't call for help?"

"Duke hurt?" Lori asked, growing increasingly agitated.

"No, honey," Ginny assured her. But all the way home from the deserted construction site, she couldn't escape the feeling that something had happened to Rick. He wouldn't have let Lori down. He'd promised.

Ginny settled Lori in with a snack and then called Uncle Emile for Rick's address.

No answer.

She powered up her computer to search the online databases. Of the twenty R. Grays listed in the

Niagara region, none lived in Miller's Bay and there wasn't a Duke Black listed anywhere. Next, she searched the online newspapers for the story of his father's death, hopeful it would mention a relative she could try.

After an hour of fruitless searching, Ginny hit upon a headline that looked promising.

Key Witness Dies after Tragic Accident. "Detective Dick White succumbed to injuries he sustained in last Tuesday's car crash, one day before he was scheduled to testify in the trial of mafia crime boss D. Delano." The article had to be about Rick's dad. The accident happened exactly the way Rick had described it, but the name wasn't right.

She pictured the torment on Rick's face as he'd recounted the accident. He'd been too deeply affected for Dick White to be some stranger Rick had picked out of a newspaper. Turning to the obituaries, she found the listing for Dick White and his wife of thirty years, Doris, survived by their son Richard.

Richard...Rick?

If he'd told her the truth, why didn't he tell her his real name?

She didn't want to believe he was still lying to her, but he sure wasn't telling her the whole truth. Ginny switched off her computer and slipped out the basement door.

The sky had bruised to a purple-blue, tinged with red.

Rick, who are you hiding from?

His tortured response when she asked him why he

never told her about her brake line echoed through her mind. *I thought I could protect you.*

Why couldn't he understand that lies hurt more than being whacked by a two-by-four?

She climbed into her car and tried his cell phone one more time.

"Hello," a tentative female voice said.

Ginny's heart thumped fast and loud and not a single word pushed past the lump in her throat.

"Hello?" The woman's voice rose.

Ginny's finger hovered over the disconnect button. Everything in her wanted to push it, but she needed the truth. "May I speak to Ri—uh, Duke, please?"

"I'm sorry, Miss Bryson, he left here hours ago."

"How do you know who I am?"

"Your name is on the call display. This is Mary Crantz, your uncle's secretary."

"What are you doing with Duke's phone?"

Mary's pause spawned a flurry of unthinkable possibilities. "I found it wedged in my sofa. Must've dropped out of his pocket. If he comes back for it, I'll let him know you called."

"No, don't bother." Ginny cranked her keys in the ignition and the already running engine squealed. She rammed her shifter into drive. "You wouldn't happen to know his address, would you?"

"Sure. He's in the apartment building on Davis Avenue."

By the time Ginny reached Rick's neighborhood, the sky was black. The frenetic hum of air conditioners filled the air. When a young couple opened the secured front door, Ginny slipped in before it closed. She scanned the board for Rick's apartment number and then took the back stairs to the third floor.

Her loud knock echoed in the tiled hallway.

Feet shuffled toward the door, but it didn't open.

She balled her hand and knocked again, harder this time.

The dead bolt clicked, followed by the rattle of a chain.

Pushing her way in, Ginny poked Rick's chest. "You have some explaining to—"

He recoiled from her touch and the words lodged in her throat. His left eye was swollen shut and the surrounding skin was five different shades of blue. His lower lip was cut and puffy, his jaw bruised.

"What happened?" She gulped in horror. She'd done it again—assumed the worst about him— when…when…someone had beaten him up.

Rick backed into the room and motioned her inside. "Robins paid me a visit."

"The guy arrested at church?"

"That's the one."

She nudged Rick toward the sofa and took in the spartan state of his apartment—white walls, bare windows, scarred hardwood floor. A laptop sat open on a wooden TV tray, and the lumpy green sofa was the only place to sit. "Lay down. I'll get you some ice."

In his freezer, the only ice available had to be chipped from the sides of the compartment. She grabbed a tea towel and a bag of frozen peas that looked like they might've been left by the last tenant.

Returning to Rick's side, she gently pressed the towel-wrapped bag against his bruised eye. When he nudged her hand aside and held the icepack in place, she couldn't stop her chin from trembling at the sight of his swollen knuckles. "Where did this happen?"

"On the street. Robins caught me by surprise." Rick growled the last part as though it seriously hurt his pride to admit.

"Have you seen a doctor?"

"Don't need a doctor to tell me I've got a cracked rib. Nothing he can do." Rick caught her hand. "I'm okay, really. I've had worse."

The stark admission froze out the warmth of his touch. She looked into his one good eye. "Who are you?"

His eye slipped shut and a long sigh seeped from his pursed lips.

Maybe pushing him, after all he'd been through tonight, was cruel. She traced the creases striping his forehead. Part of her wanted to tell him she'd read his parents' obituaries, that she knew his last name wasn't Gray, or if it was, that he'd fabricated the car accident story. But the other part of her, the part that came alive whenever he looked at her, wanted to give him the benefit of the doubt, wanted to believe he had a logical explanation, wanted to hope he'd tell her everything without being coerced.

"I was worried about you when you didn't make Lori's game. I was afraid—" Her voice cracked. He was at another woman's apartment, she reminded herself. "I tried calling your cell, but you didn't answer."

"I lost it."

"You left it at Mary's apartment."

"Oh good, that's one less thing for me to worry about." He tilted his head and studied her for an uncomfortably long time. A slow smile curved his lips. At least it looked like a smile. With the way his bottom lip bulged she couldn't be sure. "Are you jealous?"

"Should I be?"

"I went to pick up paperwork."

"It's really none of my business. It's not like we're a couple."

"Aren't we?" He curled a finger around a lock of her hair. "You are jealous."

She pulled away. "Why wouldn't Mary hand the papers to you at the door?"

"What makes you think she didn't?"

"Oh, I don't know. Maybe because your phone was wedged in her couch."

Rick actually had the nerve to chuckle. "Do you know how cute you are when you're jealous?"

Ginny sprang to her feet. "I am not jealous."

Rick caught Ginny's hand. "I'm sorry. Don't be mad."

The ache in his chest had nothing to do with his cracked ribs. After Robins finished with him, Rick had dragged himself to the first house he could reach and called Zach to keep an eye on Ginny. If Rick really wanted to protect her, he would end their doomed relationship here and now. Clearly, she'd come with that intention…until she saw his battered face.

The problem was he didn't want their relationship to end.

When she admitted she'd been worried about him, her voice cracking, he'd wished with every aching cell in his body that they could have a future together. But how could they?

Guys like Robins would always be out there, watching for a chance to take their revenge…just like they'd done to Dad. Revenge that cost Mom her life.

As long as Rick worked undercover, he would never be able to ensure the safety of anyone close to him. And that reality made him feel as bruised on the inside as out. Ginny deserved so much more than he could offer.

He'd sidetracked her who-are-you question by teasing her about being jealous, but he couldn't dodge the question forever.

"I'll fix you a cup of tea," Ginny said, extricating her hand from his hold.

His gaze followed her to the kitchenette and then drifted to the bare walls, as empty as his life had felt without her these past fifteen months. She was so compassionate and caring; she made him feel like a better man just by being near her. How could he let her go?

How could he let go of the one person who saw

through his masks to the man inside—the man who loved her like she was a part of his very being?

If he gave Ginny up, he truly would become nothing more than his job, a shell of an identity that even he didn't know anymore.

Two simple words could release him from the grip of those lies. Two simple words would free him to love her completely. Two simple words.

I quit. *I quit.* Nothing could be simpler. People quit their jobs every day.

Promise me, son. Promise me. Don't let them win.

Dad's words tore through Rick with the same terrifying force of the crash that had ripped him from Rick's life. He shielded his eyes with the bag of peas, curled his knees to his chest. How many times had he overheard Dad tell Mom, "If I quit, they win. We can't let them beat us. We owe it to Bobby." And at the mention of Rick's deceased older brother, Mom would relent.

Not once did his parents blame Rick. Not once. He swallowed the guilt that ate through his soul like cancer. He'd been too young to understand that gang members got a kick out of daring probationary gang members to take potshots at a cop's house. But if Rick had obeyed his parents and stayed in the backyard, Bobby never would've chased him to keep him off the road. Because of his defiance, his brother had run straight into the spray of gang bullets.

The ache in Rick's chest intensified.

Ginny returned with two steaming mugs.

When their gazes met, all the qualms he'd had

about pursuing a relationship with her and had ignored for the past seventy-two hours rose up and mocked him. When had his lofty dreams of making a difference in the fight against crime fizzled into disillusionment?

His gaze fell to his well-worn Bible sitting on the window ledge, where it had sat untouched for days, and the answer hit him square in the chest. Somewhere along the line his deceptions had changed who he was deep inside, as surely as his undercover identities changed who he was on the outside.

Ginny touched his arm. "Are you okay?"

He set aside the thawing bag of peas and covered her hand with his own. "Been better. I guess you won't want to be seen with this face at the fundraiser?"

She knelt beside the sofa and brushed the hair from his forehead. "You just worry about getting your strength back."

Rick kissed her palm. "I'm sorry I let you down."

Her head tilted and she gave him a confused look.

"By missing Lori's T-ball practice."

"Oh. I think I can forgive you this time." Her expression turned teasingly serious. "But don't let it happen again."

The words sliced through his cracked ribs straight to his heart. No, he wouldn't. But other promises demanded his attention, too. Laud had to have other plans for the pending fundraiser money. And it was time for Rick to up the ante.

FIFTEEN

"This is fantastic!" Kim squealed, hurrying toward Ginny as fast as her black sheath and strappy heels would allow.

Chandeliers, their crystals like floating raindrops, splashed dappled light around the room, while the guests in their glittering gowns and black tuxedos moved in and out of the shadows.

Yeah, Ginny had to admit she hadn't thought she could pull the fundraiser together, but she felt as though she'd walked into a five-star event.

Everything—from the food tables overflowing with pâté and smoked fish, croissants and mini-quiches, cheesecake and chocolate tortes, to the flamboyant wail of the sax in the jazz band—bore a feeling of opulence.

"Why are you so tense?" Kim squeezed Ginny's arm. "Relax, your job's over."

"I can't relax. I have to persuade all these people to make generous bids."

"Are you kidding me? The auction items will sell

themselves. I can't believe you scored a three-night stay at a resort in the Poconos."

"Just remember that's for married couples." Ginny inclined her head toward Zach who stood in front of a baseball poster. "Something tells me the men are more interested in bidding on the box seats to the Blue Jays game." At Kim's groan, Ginny chuckled. "At least you have a date tonight."

"I'm sorry Duke didn't come."

Ginny shrugged. Seeing Kim smitten with Zach made her yearn for Rick. That, or the heady fragrance of romance in the air, as though the hotel pumped it in through the air-conditioning vents.

"He would've looked good in a tux," Kim mused, as if she'd read Ginny's thoughts.

"Oh, yeah, he would've outclassed every man here." Not that she was comparing, because last night Rick told her he didn't feel up to attending and she should just get over the disappointment flopping in her chest.

Ginny's mother cut through the clusters of guests. "Can you believe how many people came?"

She teetered on her high heels and Ginny steadied her. "Why don't you sit at a table? There are lots of small round ones still open near the stage."

Kim winked and then scurried off.

"No, I want to look," Mom said, her words slurring.

"Have you been drinking?"

"Just a glass of punch." Mom scowled. "You mean alcohol? How could you think that?" She bent to adjust the strap on her sling-backs. "It's these heels. I'm not used to them." Before Ginny could press the matter, Mom hurried off to give Lori a hand with her food.

Putting the episode out of her mind, Ginny perused the silent auction tables. She added her bids to a few items and talked up the value of others to those browsing. Her fingers grazed the certificate for three nights at a Poconos resort…in the honeymoon suite.

"Excuse me, may I bid on the resort?"

Startled, Ginny looked up at a pretty brunette with a ballpoint pen poised in the air. Ginny smoothed out the tablecloth in front of the bidding sheet and stepped back, her gaze drawn to the star-cluster diamond ring on the woman's left hand.

Once upon a time, Ginny had pointed out a similar ring through a jewelry shop window when Rick had asked—hypothetically, of course—what kind she liked.

Ginny forced herself to look at the next item on the table. A knife set—perfect for the next time Rick wanted to stab her heart. He knew how important this night was to her, to her family. How could he bail?

Sure he'd been beat up, but his injuries hadn't stopped him from working every day, or from being too busy with *other business* every evening to see her.

Ginny tugged her shawl over her bare shoulders and shrugged off her disappointment. Except she couldn't get his blue-gray eyes out of her mind.

They'd begged her to understand, to not ask questions, to trust him. And their unspoken plea had kept her from confronting him with what she'd learned from the newspaper article.

Somehow she wound up in front of the bidding sheet for the honeymoon suite again.

A gentle hand straightened her shawl before coming to rest at the small of her back. *Rick.* Smiling, she leaned into the warm pressure. "I didn't think you were—"

"Enjoying yourself?"

"Eddie?" She stiffened. Since when had he become so…familiar?

In a black tux, he didn't look at all like the mechanic in greasy coveralls who'd sentenced her car to the scrap yard. But she hadn't given him a reason to think they were more than friends—acquaintances, really.

Thankfully, he dropped his hand and offered her a glass of punch.

Across the room, Rick stepped into view, his gaze fixed on her. A small frown tugged at the corner of his mouth as he leaned back against a table, one hand in his pocket.

Punch dribbled over her fingers. He'd come. And in that tux, with his broad shoulders, bronzed skin and two days' worth of beard growth, he looked like a movie star.

"Oops." Eddie whisked a napkin from his side pocket and traded it for the glass.

Ginny swiped at the sticky liquid and snuck another peek Rick's way. Why didn't he come over and talk to her? Had he seen her lean into Eddie's touch?

If she hadn't just been dreaming about Rick, she never would've mistaken Eddie for him. Even all snazzied up she could still catch the whiff of engine oil embedded in Eddie's skin. Whereas, even with a yellowing bruised eye, Rick looked way too good in his tux. And the amused little smile he now directed her way told her he knew how good.

"There's a car auction in Toronto on Tuesday," Eddie said, returning her glass. "I'll take you, if you like. I can help you find a replacement for your Impala."

"What a sweet offer. Thank you. But my uncle already bought me a used car."

"Oh." Eddie's shoulders drooped. "I'd be happy to check it over for you. No charge."

She nodded her thanks. He wasn't bad looking, really, and he was thoughtful and clearly interested. Why couldn't she fall for a nice, dependable guy like Eddie, instead of Rick?

Rick said something to Zach and then started toward her. Except Uncle Emile's receptionist, dressed in a shimmery black strapless dress that curved in all the right places, intercepted him.

Mary rested her hand on Rick's shoulder, tipped onto her toes and whispered something close to his ear, bringing a smile to his lips.

Ginny grimaced.

"What is it?" Eddie frowned at his glass. "Is something wrong with the punch?"

"No." Ginny blushed at being caught with her attention elsewhere. "I saw someone I didn't expect."

Eddie glanced over his shoulder. "Anyone I know?"

"No one important." Unless she counted how much she and Lori looked forward to seeing Rick at her T-ball games. Or how fiercely protective he'd become of her since the two-by-four incident. Or how much she yearned to truly know the real Rick Gray.

But how important could a man who lied to her really be?

She'd been fooling herself to think they could find a way to the truth. His lies stood like an electric fence between them. She could see the man, but every time she got close, reality jolted through her, fierce, unnerving, leaving her thrumming with frustration.

No, he couldn't be important.

She strolled along the auction tables. "Have you bid on any items?"

"Not yet." Eddie followed her a little too closely. "Any you recommend?"

"You might like the pair of baseball tickets."

"Would you go with me if I won?"

"I'm afraid coaching my sister's T-ball team is as close as I care to get to baseball. I have my eye on the pair of tickets to the Millennium Theatre in Lancaster. Have you ever been?"

"No, but I'm sure I'd love it." He steered her toward the bidding sheet with a light touch to the small of her back. "With you, that is." His tone dipped suggestively.

Guilt knotted Ginny's stomach as Eddie jotted down a bid. Her gaze strayed to where she'd last seen Rick, but he'd disappeared again.

Why should she feel guilty? Maybe Eddie was the man God had picked for her and she'd been too distracted by what's-his-name to see it.

"Are you okay?" Eddie asked.

"Sorry, I have a lot on my mind."

"Like what, Ginny? What's on your mind?" Rick practically materialized at her side, which made her wonder what other special powers he might have.

Good thing they didn't include mind reading, because right now she wanted to pour her glass of punch into that fancy suit and blurt a few choice words about his showing up unannounced after reneging on his invitation.

Except, his too-charming smile swept the words from her drying mouth.

He angled his body toward hers in a subtle attempt to shut Eddie out.

Eddie regarded him like so much bug splat on a windshield and cleared his throat. "Don't you need to place some bids?"

Rick, his gaze glued to her with unmistakable appreciation for what he saw, delayed his response a moment longer than politeness dictated. "Excuse me?"

Eddie shoved aside the flaps of his jacket and hooked his thumbs on his suspenders. "You heard me."

Lori pushed between them. "Duke. Me princess."

She twirled and her organza skirt swirled like a bright orange flower.

Rick took her hand and twirled her again, this time under his lifted arm. "You certainly are."

She beamed. "You take Gin show?"

He sent Ginny a confused look.

"She means at the Millennium Theatre. I told her I wanted to go."

He grinned at Eddie. "Excuse me, it seems I have a bid to place after all."

"Me show." Lori tugged him toward the table.

Ginny's heart thumped so loud she was certain Eddie would hear it. How could she stay mad at a guy who doted on her sister with such genuine pleasure? She offered Eddie an apologetic smile. "I'm sorry about that. Lori adores Duke, and I'm afraid he spoils her."

"She must be excited about moving into the group home."

Ginny let her gaze stray to where Lori was pointing to every other item on the auction table. "Yes, I think so."

Eddie inched closer. "You'll have more time for yourself then."

"Yes, I suppose that's true."

He reached for her hand. "I'd like to—"

"I brought you those little quiches you love so much," Rick interrupted, pressing a plate into the hand Eddie had wanted to hold.

A little stunned and immensely grateful, she followed the movement of Rick's finger above the food.

"See this one's cheese and this one's mushroom." He turned to Eddie. "I'm afraid I outbid you on those theater tickets. No hard feelings, hey?"

Eddie's hand clenched at his side. "We're here to raise money for a worthy cause."

"Right you are."

"Ginny, would you like to sit?" Eddie said, abruptly. "Listen to the band?"

"Not right now, thank you." She touched his arm to soften her refusal. "I need to have a few words with Duke."

With a begrudging nod, Eddie backed away.

Ginny turned on Rick. "What are you doing here after canceling our date?"

"I couldn't stand the thought of you being alone." Rick steered her toward a table for two. "Now, tell me. Was it just me or did Eddie treat me like a rival?"

"Rival?" Had Rick said rival? As if the possibility worried him?

She hardly noticed that her shawl had slipped off her shoulders until Rick reached out and caught it, running his palms down her arms. At his touch, her skin prickled with waves of anticipation.

Great, now her mind, heartbeat and skin had all decided that he could be forgiven for withdrawing his invitation only to show up unannounced, expecting her to fall into his arms. The next time she went out where there might be the remotest chance Rick showed up, she'd wear a wool dress with long sleeves and a high collar.

Staring at his chest, she tried to remember what they were talking about.

He settled the silky fabric around her shoulders and they sat at the quiet table. "Have you ever been out with Eddie?"

"Ooh, who's jealous now?"

Rick's tone lost its playful edge. "A thwarted Romeo might be persuaded to do something stupid."

His words took a moment to sink in. Oh. He wasn't being romantic. He was trying to figure out who might have hurt her.

Besides himself. Someone like...

"You think Eddie sabotaged my brakes?"

Her outburst set off a ripple in the crowd.

She ducked her head and her hair fell forward. She hoped it was enough to shield her from curious stares.

Rick tucked a few strands behind her ear, his eyes never leaving hers. "I'm afraid it's a possibility. Or someone might've paid him to lie about what really happened."

"Can we *not* talk about this tonight? It's bad enough I have to worry my mom will put on a lamp shade and dance on the tables without having to worry about Eddie sticking an hors d'oeuvre pick in my back."

She shrank in her seat, horrified that she'd voiced her fears.

Rick tugged the ends of her shawl. "Why would you worry about your mom acting like a drunk?"

Ginny groaned and slid her gaze in the direction she'd last spotted Mom.

Mom fluttered her hand, looking way more animated than her usual—or maybe not so usual—sober self.

Rick's hands fell to the table, leaving Ginny's shawl and emotions dangling.

What gave him the right to judge?

The band finished playing its set and she clapped much longer than necessary.

He cupped her chin and forced her to look at him. "Why didn't you tell me your mom has a drinking problem?"

Ginny jerked back. "Oh, that would've made a great topic of conversation for a date." Her voice edged higher. "Would've fit right in with 'by the way Ginny, I'm a gang lord and my real name is *Richard White.*'"

Around them the chatter stopped and a dozen pairs of eyes turned in their direction.

Well, let them stare. It was high time Rick came clean.

But for some reason, his sudden paleness didn't give her the jolt of satisfaction she'd expected.

Rick clutched Ginny's hand. "Please tell me you haven't told anyone."

"So it's true?"

He tightened his grip. "Have you told anyone?"

"No. I went to your apartment to get answers the night Robins beat you up. But—"

"Ginny, believe me. I will give you those answers. I just can't yet. Until I can, it's imperative you tell no one, not even your mom or your uncle. Do you understand?"

"I told Kim about your dad."

Rick let out a long breath, debating how much he needed to admit to allay Ginny's curiosity before it got her hurt. "I didn't lie to you about my name. I changed it legally to Rick Gray as protection from the guy behind my dad's murder."

"He came after you?" she gasped.

"Sort of." Eighteen months of solid evidence. It should've been a straightforward arrest. Instead…

In Rick's darkest moments, the guy's face still haunted him—the face of the first and only man he'd ever shot. Dead.

"There's no sort of. He either did or he didn't."

Suddenly everything Zach had said about Rick being too close to this case came into utterly painful clarity. "It's complicated. Not everything is black-and-white, Ginny. Sometimes, it's just gray."

The disillusionment in Ginny's eyes hurt bone-deep. She was a black-and-white kind of person. Actions were either right or wrong. No room for in-betweens. No allowance for a lesser evil to achieve a greater good. No excuse for lies.

Bracing his hands on the table, Rick climbed out of his emotions. "I'm sorry. I didn't mean to upset you. It must've been hard for you holding the family together when your mom drank."

Mrs. Bryson pressed her fingers to her temple and

swayed against a table, almost knocking off a platter of shrimp. Eddie caught her elbow and handed her a glass.

A disturbing hunch fisted Rick's heart. "Have you seen your mom actually drink alcohol tonight?"

"No. She got pretty good at hiding it over the years."

"How well does Eddie know your mother?" As Rick studied the pair, the fist tightened. He pulled Ginny to her feet, cutting off her response.

Eddie had his arm around Mrs. Bryson's waist and was leading her out the door.

Ginny's frown turned to alarm. "What's Eddie doing with my mom?"

SIXTEEN

Rick hurried Ginny out the ballroom doors and signaled Zach to follow. "Fan out. We need to find Mrs. Bryson before Eddie gets her out of the hotel."

If Eddie was the one who hurt Ginny, then he might've poisoned Ginny's mom or—

Rick spotted Eddie pacing a hall off the lobby and charged.

Eddie lifted his hands. "Whoa, man, am I glad to see you. We need to tell Gin—"

Rick grabbed Eddie's arm, twisted it behind his back and pushed him face-first into the wall. "Where is she?"

"What's your problem?" Eddie struggled against Rick's grip. "Let go of me."

Ginny ran up to them. "Rick, what are you doing?"

"Rick?" Eddie craned his neck. "I thought your name was Duke?"

"Where's Mrs. Bryson?" Rick growled, shoving him harder.

"In the bathroom, she—"

"Zach, over here," Rick shouted, and followed

Ginny into the women's restroom, leaving his partner to question Eddie.

Mrs. Bryson stood clutching the marble countertop, staring at her reflection in the gilt-framed mirror. The bright lights made her face look deathly pale. "My meds must…" She blinked once and then again more deliberately. "I see…double." Her words slurred and then suddenly she just crumpled.

"Mom!"

Rick lunged forward and caught Mrs. Bryson around the waist. "It's okay. I've got you. Let's get you somewhere you can lie down."

Her left eye drooped and the side of her mouth went slack.

Scooping her into his arms, Rick clenched his jaw against the scream of his cracked rib, and muscled open the door. With a lift of his chin, he summoned Zach. "We need an ambulance."

Zach whipped out his phone. Shooing aside curious onlookers, he cleared a path to the lobby. Kim hurried to Ginny's side.

Rick set Mrs. Bryson on the couch and took her hand in his. "Tell me. How does this feel?"

"Tingles."

"Your leg, too?"

"Feels—" panic filled her eyes "—gone."

Fighting his own rising panic, Rick offered a reassuring smile. "It's okay, Mrs. Bryson. Help is on its way." He turned to Zach, who was already on the line with a 9-1-1 operator. "Tell them we have a fifty-nine-year-old female cancer patient, slurring, numbness and tingling down left side, pupils are…" Rick covered both of her eyes with his palms and then lifted them away. When the pupils didn't seem to respond equally, he tried again, and then a third time, uncovering one eye at a time. "Pupils equal and reactive."

Turning Mrs. Bryson onto her slack side, Rick flicked his gaze to Ginny. She stood at the end of the couch, face whiter than her mom's, her expression terrified. He gave Zach a telling look. No need to alarm Ginny more than necessary

With a nod, Zach acknowledged that he understood.

Rick checked that Mrs. Bryson's airway was protected. Rubbing her chilled arms, he spoke in a soothing voice. She answered his questions in grunts.

Near panic, Ginny ripped away from Kim and paced in front of the glass doors. "What's taking them so long?"

Kim looked helplessly at Rick.

As much as he wanted to, he couldn't leave Mrs. Bryson's side to go to Ginny. But they had another problem, too. Curious guests were gathering in the lobby. "I need you to see to Lori. Keep her away, and after we're gone, see that she gets home. I'll take care of Ginny." Somehow.

A hotel employee hovered at the head of the couch, a cotton blanket clutched in his hands. "Sir, is there anything I can do?"

Zach snapped shut his phone and relieved the concierge of the blanket. "Yeah, you can meet the ambulance outside."

Rick slid his fingers to Mrs. Bryson's wrist to check her pulse. "Zach, what's the ETA on that ambulance?"

"Four minutes." Zach tucked the blanket around her. Jutting his chin toward Ginny, he took over monitoring Mrs. Bryson's condition.

Resisting the urge to simply fold Ginny in his arms and offer comfort, Rick pulled her toward the couch. "Honey, your mom needs you. Hold her hand and just talk to her. Assure her. The calmer she remains, the better she'll be."

Ginny's chin trembled as she reached for her mom's hand. "I'm here, Mom."

Flashing red lights came into view and the hotel employee wedged open the doors.

Ginny brushed a strand of hair from her mom's face. "Don't worry. These guys know what to do."

Rick briefed the paramedics as they wheeled in a gurney, then wrapped his arm around Ginny's shoulders and drew her out of their way.

What little color remained in her face drained as she watched the paramedics check her mom's vitals and strap on an oxygen mask.

"Your mom is in good hands. Do you want to ride in the ambulance with her?"

Ginny trembled uncontrollably and her eyes grew enormous—not the kind of calming effect the paramedics were looking for.

"It's okay. I'll drive you to the hospital." Rick turned to Zach. "Keep an eye on…things."

"Yeah, will do."

Rick hustled Ginny to his truck, thankful he'd pulled Zach in on this case. The sirens blipped. Traffic cleared and the ambulance pulled away. This wasn't how tonight was supposed to play out.

The flashing red lights of the ambulance threw a sickly light into the truck's interior. Rick reached across the seat and squeezed Ginny's arm. "You okay?"

"I accused her of drinking. One of the paramedics said Mom had a stroke, and I accused her of drinking." Ginny stared at the rear of the ambulance, her eyes glistening with unshed tears. "How could I have missed the symptoms?"

"This is not your fault."

Ginny's hands twisted in her lap. "Mom used to act that way when… How was I supposed to know? At my friend's wedding she toppled into the—" A sob cut off her words.

Rick parked outside the hospital and guided Ginny through the triage area toward Admitting. Everyone, from a sniffling toddler to an elderly man with a laceration on his forehead, stopped talking and stared as they passed.

Panic flared in Ginny's eyes. "Why are they staring at us? Mom couldn't have di—?"

"No, it's our clothes." He smiled at her green gown, shimmering under the hospital fluorescents, and inclined his head toward the desk.

A petite woman in blue scrubs greeted them. "Are you a relative of Mrs. Bryson?"

"Her daughter. How is she?"

The agony in Ginny's voice swiped Rick's breath. *Please, Lord, don't let this be the end.*

"The team is examining her now." The nurse said in a clinical tone that offered no reassurance.

Ginny pulled a crumpled piece of paper from her purse. "I have Mom's health card number and a list of her medications. She has—"

"That's fine." The nurse handed Ginny a clipboard and motioned toward a waiting room. "Write the information on these forms, then bring them to the desk."

After the glaring lights of the hallway, the dimly lit room with its cracked yellow walls and orange plastic chairs felt bleak. Rick remained standing as Ginny perched on the edge of the seat closest to the table and filled in the forms with slow precision. Her fingers turned white where they gripped the pen, and he feared she was on the edge of unraveling.

Rick ripped open the knot on his tie and tried to ignore the antiseptic odor that threatened to strangle him. He felt as helpless as the day they'd brought Dad to the hospital, his life all but gone from his body. Why couldn't the nurse at least tell them if Mrs. Bryson was stable?

The click of a pen pulled him from his thoughts. Ginny picked up the clipboard and slipped from the room without seeming to see him reach out his hand.

He waited in the doorway, but when she returned,

she shrank from his touch and moved toward the window, wrapping her shawl around herself.

"Would you like a coffee?" he asked.

Taking her shrug as a yes, he set a waxed cup under the spout and flipped the lever. The smell of coffee usually perked him up, but here, it mingled with the hospital odors and curdled his stomach. He doctored the brew with a little cream and sugar then coaxed Ginny into a chair.

She took a sip, her gaze fixed on nothing in particular.

"Your mom will be okay."

"You can't know that." Ginny spooned one, two, three spoons full of sugar into her already sweetened coffee.

He ached to take away her pain.

"Miss Bryson?" A woman in a white lab coat stood at the door.

Ginny rushed toward her. "Can I see my mom now?"

"Not yet. We have to run a few more tests first. Can you tell me how long she's displayed these symptoms?"

Ginny covered her mouth and shook her head. After a moment, her hand slid to her throat. "A few weeks ago—" Ginny let out a ragged breath "—she was unsteady on her feet, slurred speech. I thought—" Tears sprang to her eyes. "The symptoms went away. She never said she was dizzy or anything."

"Denial in a patient is natural. They don't want

to face what's happening to them. But you need to report any changes in behavior immediately, they could be a reaction to her medicines, a change in the tumor, anything. If we'd known sooner, we might have kept this from escalating."

"Escalating? What's wrong with her?"

"I'll have answers for you in a little while. You sit tight."

Ginny's panicky gaze skittered past Rick as she turned toward the darkened window. "Why didn't Mom tell me she wasn't feeling well? If she would've said something…"

"She probably didn't want to worry you."

"But I thought—" Again Ginny cupped a hand over her mouth and shook her head.

The anguish in her face tore at his heart. He moved close enough to lay his palm on her shoulder, allowing her the space she seemed to crave when everything in him wanted to pull her into his arms.

Ginny touched a finger to the windowpane. "Mom always told me I was too quick to assume the worst about people. I never believed her. But it's true."

Uncertain how to respond, Rick said nothing. He'd been on the receiving end of Ginny's judgments more than once. Although in his case, they'd always been more than justified.

Ginny drew stick people on the windowpane—two tall, two short, a family. "When I saw Mom stumble and heard her speech slur…" Ginny's voice thinned. "It was just like—" She smeared the picture with her palm. "If only I'd realized…"

Rick gently turned her into his arms. "Oh, sweetheart, this is not your fault."

"What if she doesn't make it? I can't remember the last time I told her I loved her."

"She knows."

"No. I tried so hard to show her, but I couldn't say it." Ginny sank into a chair. "I think I'd resented Mom for so long that when she finally gave up the drinking and lying I couldn't let go of those feelings."

Lying? Suppressing a groan, Rick sat beside her. *I can't love another person who lies to me.* All this time he'd thought Ginny had been talking about some guy who'd cheated on her.

"When I was a teenager, Mom insisted on driving me to my friend's house—even though she'd been drinking." Ginny's voice grew distant. "A cop—the father of my prom date-to-be—pulled us over. The next day my date canceled on me and my mom became the school joke."

Ginny curled her fingers into her shawl. "When I got home that day, I called Mom all sorts of nasty things. I blamed her for Lori's problems, my problems, even Dad's death. I was horrible."

"You were hurt and angry and a teenager. Being horrible is part of the job description."

Ginny didn't return his smile. "How could she possibly love me knowing how I felt about her?"

"We all say things we later regret. I'm sure she's forgiven you."

"I never asked her." Ginny buried her face in her hands. "I've been so blind. I tried so hard to be the daughter she wanted, to honor her like God expects, but I never stopped judging her."

"Oh, Ginny." Rick rubbed her back. "I've seen the way you cringe when your mom criticizes you, and I wonder if deep down you believe her, if you think you're not good enough somehow, and hope maybe by doing everything right, you'll make yourself worthy of her love and God's. But it won't work. We're not worthy. Not one of us. That reality makes God's gift all the more precious." Rick pried Ginny's hands away from her face. "God loves you, no matter what."

"But God hates sin." Ginny wrapped her arms around her waist. "We have to take responsibility for our actions."

"Yes, but God never stops loving us. The Bible says, 'He doesn't treat us as our sins deserve… For as high as the heavens are above the earth, so great is His love for those who fear Him.'"

"Yes, but—"

"Ginny, there are no buts. I've seen your face light up when you share God's love with one of the kids on your T-ball team. They see in you, maybe for the first time in their lives, someone who accepts them how they are. You help them believe that maybe God does, too."

Rick wiped a tear from her cheek. "Yet, sometimes I see in your eyes the same torment I've seen in the street kids at the drop-in center. Kids who never managed to earn their parent's unconditional love."

When Ginny pulled back, Rick softened his voice.

"Most people think they have to clean up their lives before God will forgive them, accept them, love them. Your head knows that's hogwash." He pressed his finger to her chest. "But your heart denies you the experience of His grace. And your mom's."

"That's not true."

"Isn't it? You need to love and accept your mom as she is—the way God accepts each one of us. You do that so easily with Lori, but with others, like your mom, you have a hard time seeing past her actions to the hurting person inside."

Ginny's face crumpled. "I hurt, too. When my dad died, I felt like I'd lost two parents." She balled her hands and scrubbed at the tears streaming down her cheeks. "After the accident at the construction site was the first time I felt like Mom really saw me as a daughter who just might need her." Pressing her palm to her chest, Ginny looked away. "And I do need her. I need her. What am I going to do if I lose her?"

Rick folded Ginny into his arms, his own heart clenched unbearably tight.

"I've taken care of Mom and Lori my whole life. When they're gone, I'll have no one. Be no one."

"That's not true." Rick cradled Ginny's head against his heart. "You'll have God and you'll have me."

She clung to him, but a voice inside of him screamed, no, she wouldn't. She wouldn't have him, or at least she wouldn't *want* him. Not once she knew who he was. And why he was really in her life.

* * *

Emile couldn't have hoped for a better turn of events if he'd arranged it himself. He smiled at Ginny's friend. Kim, wasn't it? "Don't worry about Lori. I'll take her home with me. We'll have fun. Won't we Lori?"

Lori grinned. "Fun. Me go uncle."

"Okay, sweetie," Kim said. "If that's what you want, I'm sure Ginny won't mind."

Emile took Lori's hand and led her to the collection table. "First, we have to see a lady about some money."

"Me like money."

"Me, too." He chuckled and turned to the cashier. "Miss Abram, my niece had to leave unexpectedly, so I'll take charge of tonight's proceeds."

"Certainly, Mr. Laud. I have everything tallied."

"Splendid. How did we do?"

"We raised almost twenty thousand dollars."

"Excellent." Plenty to keep Petroski off his back for another week. But Emile still couldn't afford to have Ginny look for a real job and lose the neat profit he skimmed from her royalties. He'd been poor once. Bullied by kids at school. Mocked for his secondhand clothes. Ignored by the girls. He never intended to go back to that life.

Mary approached, looking intriguingly sleek in her gown. "Is this lovely girl your niece?" She offered Lori her hand. "Hello, my name's Mary."

"Hello, my name Mary," Lori mimicked.

"Wow, what a coincidence."

Emile hugged her to his side. "Her name's Lori."

An attractive blush tinged Mary's cheeks. She was one of the loveliest secretaries he'd had in a long while—one he might want to keep if she didn't get nosy like the others.

"Here you are," Miss Abram interrupted, holding out a zippered vinyl pouch.

"Excuse us," Laud said to Mary as he took the pouch. "Lori and I need to hit the night deposit box before my princess turns into a pumpkin." He tweaked Lori's nose. "Right, sweetheart?"

She twirled, crumpling her skirt in her fists. "Me princess."

"Yes, you are."

Mary tilted her head with a wistful expression. "She adores you."

"I assure you, the feeling is mutual." He crooked his arm and Lori slid her hand through like a true princess. More than a few guests offered nods of approval as they passed.

Show compassion to the less fortunate, donate to a worthy cause, build a home for the needy and everyone thinks you're honorable. Too bad the insurance company wasn't so easily persuaded. If they'd paid the settlement on the townhouse fire instead of dragging on a fruitless investigation, Petroski would already have his money.

The moment they stepped into the cool night air, Lori burrowed into Emile's side.

He disentangled himself from her grip and laid his hand on her head. "What's the matter? Are you cold?"

"Dark."

"And you don't like the dark, huh?"

She turned her head from shoulder to shoulder.

Victorian lampposts bathed the half-empty parking lot in shadowy light, but apparently not enough light to help a giddy couple find where they'd parked, or to convince Lori not to cling.

"Look at that big moon smiling down at you," Emile said, hoping to distract her long enough to get her to his car before she threw a fit.

A shadow detached itself from the side of the building, making them both jump.

"Do you have a light?" The shadow—a young man in dark clothes—held out a cigarette.

What was he doing accosting them in the hotel parking lot? Emile wrapped a protective arm around Lori's shoulders. "Sorry, I don't smoke."

"Smoke bad." Lori coughed in demonstration.

Emile tightened his hold on the money pouch and kept Lori moving.

The man circled like a vulture. "Is that right? And who told you that?"

"Teacher said."

Muddled shadows warped the man's smirk into something more sinister.

A car door slammed. Behind them, more revelers

toppled out the lobby doors. Emile glanced their way and then gave the man a pointed look.

He backed off.

"Come along." Emile squeezed Lori's arm and steered her toward his car. "Didn't your mom teach you not to talk to strangers?"

"You talk," she protested with a stomp of her foot.

Annoyed by her insolence, he tightened his grip on her arm. "I'm older than you." He opened the passenger door and deposited Lori inside. But as Emile rounded the front of the car, he saw the man's face reflected in the windshield.

Lori screamed and Emile's eyes met hers through the glass at the same instant a blow struck him between the shoulder blades.

"What the—?" He reached for the hood. Missed and slammed his chin into the fender.

The assailant moved to his side.

"Take it easy." Emile swiped his hand across his mouth and it came away sticky. "I paid you to pretend to hurt me, not leave marks!"

Another blow, this time to the kidneys, dropped him to the pavement.

His breath puffed out. Lori's muffled screams from inside the car melded with the scuff of footsteps past his head.

The assailant tore the pouch from his grip and ran.

Staggering to his feet, Emile gritted his teeth against the pain. "Stay in the car," he shouted to Lori. He hit the power locks before loping after his assailant.

The people milling outside the hotel must've noticed the commotion. Someone would call the police. He just had to make it look good for a few more minutes.

Footsteps pounded behind him.

Oh, great. That's all he needed—some hero wannabe who might actually overtake the guy.

The thief disappeared around the corner, already fifty yards ahead of them.

Out of breath, Emile stopped and braced his hands on his knees.

Kim's date raced past. "I'll get him."

Just perfect. Emile limped toward his car. He'd been so close to having the money for Petroski, and now this.

In the distance, police sirens whirled. Kim stood outside the passenger window trying to calm his hysterical niece.

So much for his perfect witness. He'd probably have to drug her just so he could get some sleep tonight. He dug out his keys and pressed the Unlock button.

Lori tumbled into Kim's arms. "Bad man hurt uncle."

Emile glanced over his shoulder. Would his thief escape in time?

Because without that cash, he was really going to get hurt.

SEVENTEEN

"Your mom had a stroke," the doctor said as he led Rick and Ginny to Mrs. Bryson's hospital room, "but she's made a remarkable recovery."

Outside Mrs. Bryson's window, streaks of red pushed back the night. But her face was as white as the pillowcase. Her skin, almost translucent, drooped. Wires disappeared under her hospital gown, and the uneven beep of the heart monitor belied the doctor's assurances.

Ginny jerked at the sight and Rick curled his arm around her. She looked so utterly broken that he barely stopped himself from turning her into his chest, so she wouldn't have to see her mom this way.

"You can do this," he whispered, willing his strength into her, but the crack in his voice betrayed his own turbulent emotions. If only he could help her find the courage to talk with her mom, as he wished he'd done with his dad. Then maybe true healing could begin.

Silently promising to support her, he nudged Ginny toward the bed.

Ginny took her mom's hand into her own trembling grasp. "Mom?"

Mrs. Bryson's eyes fluttered open. She squinted against the light. When her gaze fell to Ginny, her lips curved into a smile.

Ginny visibly relaxed. "How do you feel?"

Mrs. Bryson's gaze touched on Rick, then darted about the room. "Where's Lori?"

Still holding her mom's limp hand, Ginny eased onto the seat next to the bed. "Kim took her home."

Mrs. Bryson shook so fiercely the bed rattled. "Does Emile know I…?"

"I'm sure he'll come by later," Ginny soothed, stroking her mom's arm.

"No!"

Ginny's gaze shot to the monitor. The line scrolling across the screen spiked erratically. "Shh, Mom, it's okay."

"Emile can't know that I almost died."

Rick rested his hand next to Ginny's on her mother's arm. "You don't have to be afraid. We're here."

"But if Emile…" Mrs. Bryson's voice quavered. "I don't want anything—" she paused to catch her breath "—to happen to Lori."

"What do you mean?" Rick fought to control his tone. "What haven't you told us about Emile?"

"I was so afraid I'd die before…"

"Before what? If you want me to help you, you need to tell me what he's threatened to do."

Ginny tried to pull Rick away from the bed. "Uncle Emile wouldn't threaten Mom."

Rick stood his ground. Mrs. Bryson knew something and he needed to know what.

"He made me promise not to tell." She took a labored breath. "Or… You can't let him take Lori."

If Rick didn't know the kind of man they were dealing with, he might have assumed Mrs. Bryson's stroke had affected her mind. From Ginny's speculative expression, she clearly did.

Unfortunately, Mrs. Bryson seemed all too rational.

"What are you afraid Emile will do?"

Mrs. Bryson tried to lift her hand, but her fingers flopped helplessly against the bedsheet. "You have to stop him."

Rick's next question lodged in his throat, caught by her look of utter desperation. "I will," he said and swallowed the truth he longed to tell them. It scraped down his throat like a chicken bone. "But I need you to tell me what he's done."

Ginny stared at Rick as if *he* belonged in a padded room. She dug out her cell phone and stalked to the window. "I'm calling home."

Mrs. Bryson ignored Rick's question and fixed her gaze on Ginny.

Kim's cheery voice chirped over the line, inviting her to leave a message.

Ginny cut off the voice and thumbed in another number, then another.

With each unanswered attempt, Mrs. Bryson grew more fidgety.

Again, Kim's recorded voice chimed into the room.

"Kim, where are you?" Ginny hissed into the phone. "Where's Lori?"

Mrs. Bryson struggled to sit up. "He has her, doesn't he?"

Rick's heart slammed against his ribs. Why would Laud take Lori? What did he have to gain? Except Mrs. Bryson's silence.

Ginny looked helplessly to Rick, an unspoken what-is-going-on question etched in her eyes.

Rick tempered the urge to whip out his own phone and call Zach. He'd left Rick a text message at 3:00 a.m. informing him everything had gone according to plan. If Lori was in danger from Laud, Zach would've said something.

Right now, Rick needed to prioritize finding out what Mrs. Bryson knew. "Why are you worried that Laud has Lori?"

Mrs. Bryson squeezed her eyes shut, but tears leaked down her leathery cheeks. "If I tell, he'll break the deal."

Rick wiped her tears with a tissue. "What deal?" His mind raced with possibilities. He should've interrogated her more thoroughly weeks ago. She'd known Laud for thirty years. In all that time, she was bound to pick up that something wasn't kosher about him.

"The…the group home."

"You think he'll destroy the group home if you tell us what you know?"

Ginny snapped her gaze to Rick's, this time clearly certain he'd lost his mind. "Uncle Emile adores Lori. Why would he destroy her home?"

"He will," Mrs. Bryson rasped. "I know…" Her voice petered out.

"What do you know?" Rick squeezed her hand. "We promise Laud won't find out."

"You have to find Lori." Mrs. Bryson pleaded.

"I will, but first I need to know—"

"No." Her head sank into the pillow from the effort of blurting out the single word. "No time. Find her."

Rick turned to Ginny. "Stay here until I get back. Whatever you do, don't let her out of your sight."

Rick blew out of the hospital parking lot and punched in Zach's number. If he could convince Mrs. Bryson to talk, she might be just the witness they needed to crack this case. But that wasn't going to happen until he found Lori.

Before Rick had a chance to ask about Lori, Zach started a rundown on last night's sting. "Mary's tip that Laud intended to stage a robbery was dead on. Our guys grabbed the punk a couple of blocks from the hotel."

"Laud doesn't know?"

"Nope. He's been phoning the kid's cell phone every ten minutes, but hasn't been stupid enough to leave an incriminating voice message. So far, the kid's not cooperating, but we think he'll change his mind."

"Has Petroski made any moves?"

"You bet. The robbery made the front page of this morning's paper. Petroski called Laud before the ink was dry. From the insinuations zinging over the wiretaps, he thinks Laud planned the robbery and wants his money. Laud—honestly, as it turns out—is saying he has no money."

Rick pulled onto Maple Street. "Does he think the kid double-crossed him?"

"That's what we're telling the kid. Laying it on thick. Speculating about what a guy like Laud does to kids who double-cross him. Sooner or later he'll crack."

"What did you tell Kim?"

"I didn't have to tell her anything. I tried to chase down the guy and now I'm her hero."

Rick didn't have to hear the grin in Zach's voice to know how good that felt. After hours of feeling like he could do no right trying to comfort Ginny, he'd been ready to slay dragons if that's what it took before she finally let herself lean on him. Of course, even if he found Lori, saved the group home and nailed Laud, once Ginny found out how much he'd kept from her, his iffy hero status would be obliterated. "Where's the money now?"

"Drake locked it up. After Laud goes down, we'll announce its recovery. And get this. The labor board is sending an inspector to the construction site Monday morning to investigate Ginny's accident."

"You didn't call them?"

"No way. And blow the trial with allegations of entrapment?"

"We're okay then. Better than okay. A hefty fine is the final push Laud needs. Time for me to offer him some alternatives. Where is he now?"

"Home."

"Okay, first I need to take Lori to see her mom." Rick swerved onto Maple Crescent, thudding over the curb. "I think Mrs. Bryson knows something that can help us put Laud away, but she won't talk until she knows Lori is safe."

"Do you think Laud poisoned her?"

"The doctors claim she had a stroke, but it's an angle worth checking. Find out what drugs mimic the symptoms." Rick pulled into the Bryson's driveway.

Kim's car wasn't there.

"Zach, do you know where Kim took Lori? Mrs. Bryson practically freaked when we couldn't get a hold of them by phone."

The line went silent.

"Zach, where's Lori?"

Ginny buttered Mom's toast in an attempt to conceal her unease over how long Rick was taking.

"Do you plan to keep Rick this time?" Mom asked.

Good question, but now wasn't the time for a conversation about Rick. He'd begged her not to reveal his true identity. Said his life could be in danger. If the mafia was still after him, she couldn't blame him for wanting to keep the truth from her, but how could she date a man dodging a death threat?

"The question was not supposed to be rhetorical."

Startled out of her thoughts, Ginny dropped the knife, streaking butter down her dress. She dabbed at the stain with a napkin. "There are things about Rick you don't know."

"I know he cares for you deeply. You need to look at his heart."

"It's not that easy." Ginny took the plastic lid off the mug of hot water as her mind replayed Rick's admonishment. *You need to love and accept your mom as she is, the way God accepts each one of us*—Rick, too. "He lied."

"How many times have you let people believe you had a normal, happy childhood?"

Ginny focused on bobbing the tea bag in the mug. "That's different. I didn't set out to deceive anyone."

"No, but people made assumptions and you chose not to correct them."

"Of course I chose not to correct them. Have you forgotten what happened when Mrs. Callaghan questioned your competence to care for Lori? Social Services wouldn't return her to our home for three whole weeks!" Ginny yanked out the tea bag and plopped it on the edge of the tray.

She may be judgmental, but she wasn't a liar. How could her mom possibly understand how it felt to be the daughter of the town drunk?

The jokes. The innuendoes.

And when did this become about *her*? They were talking about Rick.

"The Bible says love covers over a mul-ti-tu... mul-ti..." Mom slumped against her pillow and let out a frustrated sigh.

"Love covers over a multitude of sins," Ginny said, finishing the verse.

"Yes." Mom tilted her head toward Ginny, resting her cheek on the pillow. "I know you pretended because you wanted to protect me and Lori, not just yourself."

Ginny's hand stilled. Mom spoke as if she loved Ginny for protecting them when all these years she'd thought Mom resented her.

Mom's eyes slipped shut. "You need to trust Rick despite the way things appear. Appearances aren't always what they seem. Look at your uncle."

"Uncle Emile is a respected member of the community. Maybe he wasn't always there for us, but he's trying to make amends."

"Your uncle…" Mom's voice dropped off. "Emile is Lori's father."

Ginny's breath stalled in her throat. A memory hovered just out of reach. Voices. Lori as a baby, crying, and Ginny trying to keep her quiet.

Ginny curled her fingers into the bedsheets.

"It happened when your daddy was on a tour of duty. You spent the night at a friend's house, so I went to visit my sister. Only she wasn't home."

Ginny uncurled her fingers. Straightened Mom's sheets.

"Emile invited me in anyway, and offered me a drink. Back then, I rarely drank and the glass of wine went straight to my head."

Seeing Mom's clothes mussed in a bag, Ginny pulled them out and began to refold them.

"Four weeks later, I found out I was pregnant. Until then, I hadn't been sure we'd actually…"

The folds of Mom's dress slipped from Ginny's fingers. Acid scorched her throat. He… He… Ginny swallowed and the pain burned clear to her soul.

I'd never marry you. You wanted me to kill her. Mom's voice, low and resolute, had crept down the hall and under Ginny's door.

The horror of that night returned full force. Ginny had scarcely been able to make out the man's words, let alone put a face to his voice, but for months afterward, she'd been too frightened to let any man near her baby sister. Then slowly her anxiety had faded, until she'd forgotten that night completely.

Or, not exactly completely. Just pushed back so far she could pretend it forgotten. "He didn't want you to go through with the pregnancy, did he?"

"No, he didn't."

Ginny crushed the dress to her chest. She might never have had a sister if her mom hadn't stood her ground. "I'm proud of you, Mom."

"I was a coward. When my sister died in the house fire, your daddy was given a two-week leave. After he shipped out, I told him I was pregnant. Naturally, he thought the baby was his. He never learned the truth."

Ginny closed her eyes. She'd always thanked God for those last two weeks with Dad.

"After your dad died, Emile thought I'd fall into his arms."

"But why, if he hadn't wanted Lori?"

"His precious reputation. If the truth came out that Lori was his, people would figure out she was conceived a month before my sister died, and might wonder if he deliberately set the fire to get rid of her."

Ginny's heart jolted. "Did he?"

"I didn't think so then, but now I'm not so sure."

The threads of Mom's story tangled in Ginny's mind, knotting into a ball of confusion. "So this is the secret you weren't supposed to tell anyone?"

"I blackmailed your uncle into building the group home so Lori would be taken care of after I was gone. I knew he wouldn't take care of her otherwise."

"Mom, I would've taken care of Lori."

"I know, honey, but I couldn't ask you to sacrifice your future."

Warmth trickled into the hollow places in Ginny's heart. Mom believed in her. Wanted the best for her. Like a real mother.

"I still don't understand what hold you have over Uncle Emile. Surely after all these years no one would assume he'd started the fire that killed Aunt Betty."

"There were other fires. Your uncle turned my sister's life insurance money into a booming business. It gave him ideas."

Ginny gasped. "You think he torches his own buildings for the insurance?" Could he really be that corrupt?

"Before that townhouse fire, Emile refused to build the group home. But when I confronted him afterward with my suspicions, he couldn't start construction fast enough. So you tell me."

"Mom, a man and woman died in that fire. If what you say is true—" Words left her as the horrible truth sunk in.

"Emile murdered them."

Ginny clutched the edge of the bed. "We have to go to the police."

"No." Mom's sharp response pinged off the walls. "This way is better—now Lori will have a home. We'll go to the police after the group home is built. Lori needs to be taken care of first."

Ginny stared at her mom in disbelief. What would the police say after so much time elapsed? She clasped her head, unable to believe Uncle Emile capable of murder.

"I'm sorry. I shouldn't have dragged you into this."

Ginny pulled Mom into her arms. "It's okay."

But it wasn't.

How could it be?

Her mother had lied to her for years. Uncle Emile wanted to kill, and now—what?—steal her sister. He might even be a murderer.

No, their lives would never be okay.

The door clicked shut. Mom stiffened. A familiar scent irritated Ginny's nose, and her heart reared.

EIGHTEEN

Uneasy about Laud being alone with Ginny and her mom, Rick tried to hurry Lori down the hospital corridor. She leaned heavily on him, her steps uncoordinated.

Would Ginny realize Lori had been drugged?

When Rick arrived at Laud's house, he hadn't been surprised to find Lori still in bed. One look at her disconnected gaze had alerted him to the truth. The fact she didn't launch herself into his arms had sealed it.

He'd scrounged every last ounce of self-control not to haul Laud off to jail then and there. His gut told him Laud had merely doped Lori so he could get a good night's sleep, but Rick would get Mrs. Bryson's consent for a doctor's exam to confirm it.

He pushed open the door to Mrs. Bryson's room and the sight of Ginny's chalky hue cut him off at the knees. "What's wrong?"

Lori tumbled into her mother's arms while Laud stood stiffly by, watching the interplay between mother and daughter.

Ginny clung to Rick and buried her face in his chest.

Hiding his surprise, Rick wrapped his arms around her and exulted in her heart-melting trust.

Laud soon made his excuses and left.

Rick nudged Ginny's chin. "Hey, what's the matter?"

She drew in a shuddery breath. "I thought Uncle Emile... Oh, I don't know what to believe. Mom told me things about him. Horrible things."

Tucking Ginny against his side, Rick nodded to the nurse he'd asked to speak to Mrs. Bryson about Lori, and then he led Ginny across the hall to an empty waiting room. He urged her to sit and took her hands in his. "Talk to me."

With halting reluctance, Ginny detailed her mom's accusations against Laud. With each revelation, Ginny shook her head as if hearing the allegations repeated made them sound too unbelievable.

Rick couldn't have hoped for a more opportune moment to tell her who he really was and why he was here. Surely she'd forgive him once she realized how necessary his secrets had been.

"Then Uncle Emile was there in the room," Ginny whispered. "He closed the door, and I was afraid he heard Mom's confession."

Rick's heart raced over this newest threat. Somehow he needed to find out what, if anything, Laud overheard. Rick didn't dare risk disclosing his true occupation now. Ginny might crack under Laud's interrogation and three months of work would be lost. Worse than that, Laud, knowing how Rick felt about

Ginny, might use her as leverage to force him to back down.

"You must think I'm overreacting." Ginny palmed the tears from her eyes, smearing her mascara. "Mom's been on a lot of meds. She's probably confused."

"I don't think so." Rick grabbed a tissue and dabbed the blackness from her cheeks. If only the lies he'd told were as easy to erase. "I haven't wanted to say anything because of how much you care for your uncle, but he has cut corners on this project and made a couple of less than ethical decisions. I think we need to be concerned about whether or not he heard your mom divulge these allegations.

"Right now your uncle trusts me and if I'm going to find out who's really behind the attacks on you and on the group home, and whether they're even connected, I need to keep his trust. But I won't have it if he doubts your loyalty."

"What can I do?"

"Find out what he heard." Rick wished there was another way, but if by chance Laud hadn't overheard anything, Ginny was the only person who could feel him out without raising alarm bells. Besides, the job was minimally dangerous, and once Rick was assured of Laud's continued trust, he could proceed with his plan.

"How am I supposed to do that?"

"Talk to him. Act like nothing has changed between you. Tell him how worried you are about your mom and how grateful you are that he's here for you.

That way, if he overheard, hopefully he'll assume you didn't believe your mom. It's crucial you don't give him any reason to think you might turn against him, okay?"

"I don't think I can. He—"

The way Ginny shook her head—as if she'd held back something too painful to voice—crushed Rick's chest with the weight of a truck. "What is it?"

Ginny shot a wary glance toward the door and lowered her voice. "Uncle Emile is Lori's dad."

Rick drew in a sharp breath. "You had no idea?"

"None. Now I understand why Mom was always so bitter toward him."

"This is not a problem. Naturally you're upset about your mom's stroke. That explains any unusual reaction you might've had to his arrival. You have to make him believe that you still trust him."

Rick hated to see Ginny strung out like this. He was getting further and further from the hero he hoped to be. But he didn't want his worst nightmares coming true at Ginny's expense. He needed her to do this, because if Laud suspected Mrs. Bryson revealed his secret, no one was safe.

Laud held the glowing tip of his cigarette to the corner of the grand-opening flyer Ginny had left behind. If she knew what he had planned, she wouldn't have wasted her time.

The paper smoked.

He'd expected Ginny to be more upset about the

theft of their funds, but her preoccupation with her mom was understandable...perhaps.

The salesman blathered over the speakerphone as flames raced along the flyer's edge.

Laud watched the words blacken, fascinated by the colors the ink gave to the flames. Just before the fire reached his fingertips, he dropped the paper into a metal wastebasket.

The salesman rambled on about how staging an untraceable fire took time, when all that mattered was the viability of the automatic sprinkler system scheduled to go into service on Wednesday. The fire had to occur before then, or the damage wouldn't be extensive enough.

Laud swiveled his chair to gaze out the window behind his desk. He'd been shortsighted to resort to hiring a young thug to pretend to rob him. Thugs couldn't be trusted. Men with families, they could be relied upon.

"Enough," he shouted. "The job will be done Tuesday night at precisely seven o'clock, or you'll never work in this county again."

"Hey, I didn't sign on for this."

"Wrong answer, Mr. Jones. You already jeopardized my operation once with your *independent thinking*."

"What are you talking about? Look how many leases I sold after I torched that other guy's building. I did that for you."

"You did that to salvage your job from your incompetence. If you play with fire, you'd better be prepared to live with the consequences. I hear the police are offering a reward for information about that arson."

"Okay, okay. I'll do what you want."

"Tuesday, Mr. Jones. I have debts to pay, too." Regardless of *who* got in the way.

NINETEEN

From the safety of her car, Ginny scanned the group home's second-story windows. She hadn't been here since the two-by-four incident and the return was more unnerving than she'd anticipated. Of course, Rick's continuous cautions didn't help. But thanks to him, the group home would open ahead of schedule despite all their financial setbacks.

Ginny tucked the stack of grand-opening flyers she wanted to show Rick under her arm and hurried inside.

The sight of the newly finished fireplace in the great room swept the breath from her lungs. The reclaimed brick, complemented by the taupe walls, added rustic warmth.

A sound rumbled through the heat vent, and her pulse quickened in anticipation. Rick had been so pleased with her success in convincing Uncle Emile of her loyalty that he'd predicted they'd snare their saboteur by week's end. With a skip in her step, she headed for the basement stairs, but the sound of a different voice stopped her short.

"The fines will bankrupt me."

Uncle Emile? His car wasn't in the driveway.

"Where do these bureaucrats come up with these numbers?"

Ginny paused at a heat vent to eavesdrop.

"So what'll you do?" Rick asked.

"I can't declare bankruptcy. My niece has her heart set on this home."

A slap sent the metal ducts into a shuddering clatter.

Ginny reared back, heart pounding. *Please, Lord, Uncle Emile's trying to do a good thing here for Lori. Please, don't make her pay for his mistakes.*

"But what choice do I have?" Uncle Emile went on, his voice uneven. "My insurance premiums will skyrocket, and with this market slump…"

Unable to make out Rick's response, Ginny dropped to her knees and pressed her ear to the vent.

"I heard the developer in Harbor Creek got a healthy insurance payout for that arson."

Ginny gasped. Was Rick suggesting what it sounded like he was suggesting?

Uncle Emile gave a disgusted snort. "The time needed to rebuild will set him back months. The payout won't come close to recouping lost revenue. Then again…" Uncle Emile's voice trailed off.

No, please don't reconsider. Ginny strained to hear his words over the thunder of her heart. After everything she'd told Rick about Mom's allegations, how could he suggest such a thing?

"…have experience?"

"You heard about the Castleman fire last summer?" Rick asked, casually.

"Sure. They never caught the guy. It cost the insurance company hundreds of thousands."

"Yup."

Ginny's throat squeezed. Rick said *yup* like he was taking credit for the job.

The stack of flyers spilled from her arms. Rick couldn't be an arsonist. He couldn't. He'd warned her to be careful, said he wanted to protect her. She gulped in a breath and tried to rationalize what she'd heard.

But she couldn't rationalize it. She couldn't. The room started to blur, along with her dreams for their future. He'd lied. Everything he said was one big lie.

At the sight of Ginny descending the basement stairs, Rick felt the blood drain from his face.

"Tell me what I heard wasn't what it sounded like," she demanded.

Summoning all the acting skill he possessed, Rick cupped her face in his hands. Everything in him wanted her to believe in the real him, the man inside. He should've known it would come down to this. If he didn't want to blow the operation, he had to stick to the lie. No matter how much she'd loathe him. "Trust me. I only have your best interests at heart."

"Trust you? You've lied to me from the first day we met."

Her words riddled his chest with bullet force and

only years of having to conceal his true emotions en-
abled him to absorb the impact with scarcely a flinch.
"Ginny, please."

She thrashed her arms and swirled free of his hold.
"Did you or did you not just offer to torch one my
uncle's buildings?"

Rick clenched his jaw, barely able to look at the
wretched pain behind Ginny's glare. He'd strung
her along. Forced her to work with him. Practically
courted her. For what?

To pluck one more criminal off the street.

No, not just a criminal.

A murderer. Tom's murderer.

"Go home, Ginny. You heard wrong." He gentled
his voice. "I'd never do anything to hurt you."

"Oh, that's rich. Do you even know the meaning
of the word? Because you throw that I-would-never-
hurt-you line around a lot. You don't have a clue how
many ways you've hurt me."

Laud caught Ginny's arm. "My dear, you needn't
concern yourself with these matters. I have no intention of taking Duke up on his rather…unusual suggestion. You misunderstood. We'll figure out a way
to make sure Lori can keep her home. Let me speak
with my banker again. I'll call you later."

Uncertainty about Laud's trustworthiness flitted
across Ginny's face. But, apparently, she trusted him
more than Rick, because she said, "Okay," and then
nailed Rick with one last scathing glare. "But I don't
ever want to see *your* face again."

Rick tried not to let that dig into his soul. His only

consolation was that Laud wouldn't mistake Ginny for his betrayer now.

"Why didn't you stop her?" Laud fumed.

So focused on keeping up the lie, Rick failed to realize that Laud would expect him to retract it in front of Ginny. Rick slipped his hand inside his leather jacket and switched on his digital recorder. He had to maintain the pretense a little longer. If Laud took the bait, he'd be behind bars by suppertime. "Do you think she would've believed me?"

"No, probably not." Laud chuckled. "Do you think she believed me?"

Rick caught himself before his frown reached his lips. "Yeah, you, I think she believed." He'd been a fool to think he could make a relationship with Ginny work. But every time he'd held her soft face in his hands, his dreams had taken over. Dreams of coming home to a wife who could make him forget the scum he mixed with on the streets every day.

Dreams that leeched away as he waited for Laud to lead the conversation back to their earlier discussion. Ginny didn't need a man who couldn't tell her where he was working for the day. Who might not be able to call if he'd be late. Who'd come home smelling like a swill because he'd doused his clothes with whiskey.

Perspiration beaded Laud's forehead and his suit didn't look its usual crisply ironed self. Maybe his conscience had finally gotten to him, too.

Rick climbed halfway up the stairs. "What was the problem you'd wanted to show me?"

"Your crew left rags and half-empty cans of paint down here. It's a fire hazard."

"We wouldn't want that. Would we?" Rick smirked.

Laud rested a foot on the bottom stair and scratched the handrail with his fingernail. "There's one more job you can do for me."

"Oh?"

"It'd be off the record." Laud half smiled—an eerie imitation of the real thing. "Insurance work."

Rick hid a smile. "Are you sure that's what you want?" He didn't bother to remind Laud what Ginny might do. He'd make sure things never got that far.

"Yeah, I'm sure." Laud's answer was too quiet for the recorder to pick up.

Rick descended a couple of steps. "What changed your mind?"

"Ginny. Until I get my creditors off my back, my family will never be safe."

"You think she'll see it that way?"

"Not a chance. But I know how to handle her."

The possible consequences of that reality twisted Rick's insides, but he kept his game face firmly intact. "I wish I did. So what'll it be? Your office building?"

"This one."

"The group home?" Rick's voice shot up. He hauled it down to a growl. "How can you ask me to burn the group home after you just said Lori—"

"This is strictly business. Do you want the job or not?"

"I can't do that to Ginny. She'd never forgive me."

Laud tilted his head, showing surprise at Rick's refusal. "Apparently, she never intends to forgive you no matter what you do."

Rick scraped his hand over his jaw, trying not to let on how deep that fact cut. "What are you paying?"

"A thousand now. Another thousand after the job's done."

Rick let out a snort. "If that's the best you can offer, you'd better do the job yourself."

"I'm a businessman, not an arsonist."

So that's how he slept at night? Strictly business. "Ten minimum," Rick said. "Setting fires is risky business."

"It has to look like an accident."

Good, Laud was determined. Maybe Rick could extract a confession yet. "No problem there. What's your usual M.O.?"

Laud cleared his throat. "I've never done this before."

"If you can't trust me enough to be honest with me, you'd better find someone else for the job."

"Okay, okay. I've had a few contractors who were—shall we say—careless. I discovered it can be a lucrative business during a market slump."

Rick nodded, moved forward a bit to encourage Laud to keep talking. "Yeah, the market's in a real slump these days. But you'd have no trouble renting these units. The government will subsidize them."

"The government has threatened to withhold final approval of the group home's status because of insufficiencies."

"But if the building burns down, you'll have your money back. No questions asked." Rick hated to float such leading statements, but he needed more from Laud.

"So will you do it?"

"When?"

"Today. There could be a problem with the propane."

"Hmm. You ever have trouble with propane before?" Rick needed names, other jobs, properties, hired thugs, methods.

"No, I've had a couple of electrical fires, spontaneous combustion of greasy rags, a carelessly discarded cigarette, that sort of thing."

"It's a wonder the insurance companies haven't written you off. Someone who hires such shoddy contractors has got to be a poor risk."

"Yes, well, I have so many different numbered companies they haven't caught on yet." His gaze shifted, suggesting that wasn't entirely true.

Rick smiled inside. He had almost enough. All he needed now was the money. "Are we agreed on the price?"

Laud pulled out his wallet and counted two thousand dollars in hundred dollar bills. "I'll give you two grand now and the other eight after the insurance company cuts the check."

Rick felt like he was shaking hands with the devil

himself, but he finally had what he needed. He twisted Laud's arm behind his back and slapped a handcuff onto his wrist. "You're under arrest for the—"

Laud drove his foot into Rick's knee.

Rick stumbled down a couple of steps and grappled for a handhold as Laud's elbow connected with his chin. Grasping only air, Rick lost his footing. The room turned circles around him. Then he ground to a halt. His head smashed against the floor and everything went black.

Laud slammed the door shut. Leaning against it, he listened for sounds of Rick stirring. When he didn't hear anything, he opened it again and peered down. Rick lay slumped face-first at the bottom of the stairs. Blood trickled across the cement.

"Are you okay, *Duke?*" Laud inched down the stairs. "Or should I call you Detective Gray? Did you really think I wouldn't figure it out?"

When Rick didn't respond to Laud's goading, Laud nudged him with his toe. "You shouldn't have done it, Detective, trying to frame me for a fire you set." Laud rummaged through Rick's pocket for the handcuff key, unlocked the one bracelet he'd managed to snap shut, then twirled them around his finger. "You won't need these anymore, and we wouldn't want the fire marshal to happen upon them." He rifled through Rick's jacket until he found the recorder he'd heard click on.

"It's too bad you're so vindictive you had to get

back at my niece for not loving you by torching her beloved group home."

Laud grabbed a wrench from behind the furnace and loosened the fitting on the propane line. "You're not very good at this arson business. Opening a gas line, thinking you could get out before a spark set it off. But you forgot the basement door self-closes and, well, that lock has always been temperamental. Cheap hardware, you know?" Laud laughed.

When the smell of gas seeped into the room, he hurried to the stairs. "Yes, you ran up the stairs trying to escape, but were soon overcome by the fumes and fell to the floor. So sad. A nasty way to die."

Laud dashed up the stairs two at a time, smashed the lightbulb at the top then slammed the heavy steel door shut. First ensuring the lock was secure, he set the timer for the overhead lights to come on at six-fifty—early enough to catch his useless salesman unaware and time enough for Rick to rue the day he thought he could double-cross Emile Laud.

He chuckled. The timer would switch on the light. The broken bulb would spark.

And kaboom.

Bye-bye Rick Gray.

Bye-bye Mr. Jones—disgruntled ex-employee.

Laud let himself out the side door and headed across the lawn to where he'd parked his car on the side street.

A thrill tingled down his spine as the sun, like a blazing ball, touched the lake and seemed to set it on fire.

TWENTY

Surrounded by a ten-foot fence, its barbs silhouetted against the gray sky, Ginny pounded on the front door of the detention center—the kind of place Rick might end up if Ginny went to the police with what she'd heard. How could he quote Bible verses to her one week and offer to torch a building the next?

Kim took one look at Ginny and joined her outside. "What's wrong?"

"I don't know what to do. My uncle's broke and… and…" Her breaths sputtered out one on top of the other. "Duke offered to burn down one of his buildings so Uncle Emile can collect the insurance money."

"No way. Duke wouldn't do that. His best friend's a cop."

"I heard him."

"You actually heard him say he'd set fire to a building?"

"Well, not exactly. He implied it. And he didn't deny it when I confronted him."

Kim rubbed Ginny's arm reassuringly. "Your uncle would never agree to such a ludicrous idea."

"No, don't you see? Mom thinks Uncle Emile has done this before. And he's desperate for cash. What if he thinks over Duke's offer and goes for it?"

"Talk to your uncle. Assure him you'll help raise the extra money he needs."

"What about Duke?" Ginny twisted her hands so hard her fingers went numb. If she wanted to do the right thing, she needed to forget how safe she felt in his arms. Forget how special she felt when he looked at her like she was the most precious person in the world. Forget the pain she'd seen in his eyes when he begged her to believe that he'd never do anything to hurt her. "I have to tell the police what I heard."

Skepticism colored Kim's gaze.

"What if he burns down another building and I never said anything?"

Kim gave Ginny a shake. "What if they were joking around? You're upset. Isn't it possible you took what you heard out of context?"

"If they were joking, do you think they would let me leave so upset?" She'd been a fool to think someone who changed his name as often as he changed jobs would change for her. She'd let Rick sneak under her defenses and dig his way back into her heart, and the gaping hole he'd left behind was swallowing her from the inside out.

"I can't believe I let myself trust him again. What is wrong with me?"

Kim caught Ginny's face between her palms. "There is nothing wrong with you. But you need to calm down and think this through. A man who stops an abusive husband from kidnapping his kid does not turn around and offer to torch a building."

Ginny's cell phone rang. She scrubbed her eyes and looked at the screen. *Laud Developments.* She gave Kim a hopeful glance and clicked Talk. "Uncle Emile?"

"No, this is Mary. Your uncle asked me to call you. He'd like you and your sister to meet him at the group home this evening at 6:45. Can you make it?"

"Yes, of course. I'll be there."

"Don't forget to bring Lori. He said it's important."

"I won't. Thank you." Ginny closed her phone and frowned at Kim. "My uncle wants to meet with Lori and me."

"That's great. You'll have a chance to clear the air."

Would she? How could she trust him after everything Mom told her?

She had to be the lousiest judge of character on the planet. She'd been wrong about...everyone. But this time, she'd find out the truth once and for all.

Rick slowly became aware of a strange odor, like rotten eggs or something that died.

He coughed and pain shot through his ribs. He pushed himself to his hands and knees and more pain exploded in his right knee. The room swayed. Seeing blood on the cement floor, he touched his head. His fingers came away wet and sticky.

Then everything came back to him in a rush— Laud, the basement of the group home...gas.

Rick bolted to his feet and grabbed the banister

for support. The room raced around him. He pulled himself up the stairs, finding it easier to breathe with each step out from under the invisible gas blanketing the floor. A few more seconds and he may never have walked out of there.

At the top of the stairs glass crackled under his feet. The door wouldn't budge. Ignoring the pain screaming through his body, he gave the door a hard shove. Nothing.

He pulled his gun out of his ankle holster and aimed at the lock.

No, the blast might ignite the gas. Is that what Laud had counted on?

Rick stumbled down the stairs and shoved open the first window he came to, then the next and the next. Life-giving air swept into the room. He filled his lungs, wishing he were half his size and could crawl through the opening.

The sound of a woman's voice jolted through his fuzzy brain. "Rick, where are you?"

"Hey, down here. In the basement."

The sound drifted away. Had he imagined it?

He glanced from window to window, but couldn't spot any movement in the deepening shadows. "Is anybody there? I need help." He reached for his cell phone, but he'd left it on the charger in his truck.

Scanning the room, he spotted the broken valve and tried to wrench it closed, but it was too badly damaged. He staggered back to the window and took another gulp of air.

With his shirt over his mouth and nose, he waded

back into the gas and shut off the main switches on the furnace and hot water tank. What else might ignite the gas?

His gaze shot to the glass at the top of the stairs. Bare filament wires dangled from the light socket above. Laud wouldn't go to all this trouble and not have that light on a timer to spark a fire unless he thought Rick was stupid enough to flip a switch.

The breaker panel. Where was it?

Rick pressed his fingers to his forehead trying to remember. The service closet, main floor.

He had to get out of here. Now.

Rick limped back to the window and shoved his face against the screen. If he didn't get out of here, his lies will have been for nothing. Nothing. And they'd cost him everything, because he'd been a liar on all fronts—not just in his job, but with Ginny. Now, she'd never know how much he loved her. With every breath.

He cringed at the memory of her saying she could never marry a cop. He'd pushed that conversation to the darkest corner of his mind, refusing to believe she wouldn't somehow change her mind. How was he supposed to convince himself he could live without her, when every thought about his future included her in it?

He wanted her beside him, always. He'd known it from the day she careened back into his life in that beat-up old car and didn't give him up to her uncle. She had every reason not to trust him. Yet, despite her fears, she'd given him chance after chance to make it right.

And he'd withheld the one truth he'd been at liberty to tell her, the truth that might have cemented her trust when everything around them crumbled.

He loved her.

His head dropped back against the cold block wall. Everything inside him hurt. He didn't deserve her. A woman who poured her heart and soul into everything she did. A woman who loyally stood by those she loved no matter how many times they wronged her. A woman whose trust he'd callously betrayed.

For what?

So he could add another notch to his belt? Be the hero? Who was he kidding?

He'd have protected her with his life, but he hadn't loved her enough to give her what she needed most. The truth.

Instead, he'd held her in his arms, kissed her sweet lips, offered his protection and begged for her trust. *Protection*. Right. He was a heartless, selfish jerk who couldn't have hurt her worse if he'd pulled out his gun and shot her straight through the heart.

He had to get out. If only to tell her the truth.

Remembering the giant cold-air return grill in the floor of the back passageway, he traced the duct to the far end of the basement, and then used the butt of his gun to hammer out the metal ties that linked each section. Next, he piled two sections together and climbed on top. The metal buckled under his weight, but it gave him enough height to reach the grill. Knocking it off, he reached his fingers over the lip of the main floor. As he kicked to push himself up, the ducts clattered away from his feet. His fingers started to slip.

He dug in and wedged one knee against the floor joist. A flash of pain almost stole his hold. Biting down a yelp, he leveraged himself against the joist and pushed himself higher until his elbows rested on the floor.

"Rick!" Mary sprinted down the hall and grabbed his arms.

"Mary? What are—?" The intensifying odor cut off his question. "Help me, quick. There's a gas leak."

She tugged on his arms while he pushed with his knee, then finally his feet, and sprawled into a heap on the hall floor. Mary yanked his arm. "Come on. We have to get out of here."

"I have to check for a timer. Go turn off the propane." Without waiting for her answer, Rick yanked his shirt over his mouth and headed for the service panel. His shoe skidded on a mess of scattered papers. The grand-opening flyers. Ginny must've dropped them. After he took care of Laud, he'd find her and tell her the truth.

Inside the service panel, a timer—set to switch on in just over an hour—was connected to the breaker for the basement lights. Rick ripped it from the box. If Laud wanted to take him out, he shouldn't have given himself so much time to get away.

Rick staggered outside, braced his hands on his

thighs and gulped in the air. His head throbbed. His knee throbbed. His heart…

No, not his heart. Ginny's rejection had ripped it out of his chest. He hobbled toward Mary. "How did you find me?"

"I saw your truck and thought I'd check out the place everyone is talking about." She waved her hands. "Never mind that. What happened to you?"

"We've got him, Mary."

"Got who?"

"Laud. Attempted murder and arson. He confessed to the fire that killed Tom."

"He confessed? To killing Tom?" Her body trembled.

Rick pulled her into his arms. "I'm sorry I couldn't tell you. But you helped bring him to justice, Mary. Tom would be so proud of you." Holding her upper arms, Rick stepped back. "Are you okay to drive yourself home? I need to call this in, find Laud and arrest him."

She managed to smile, her eyes awash with grim satisfaction. "Yes, go."

Rick turned to his truck. Mary was a strong woman. She'd get through this. With one last glance behind him, he climbed inside and then raced toward Laud's office.

TWENTY-ONE

In the dwindling light, shadows carved strange features across the walls, making the group home look almost creepy.

Or perhaps the effect was from the blight Rick had forever stamped on his work.

Ginny's heart flopped in her chest as she grabbed the list of charitable foundations she'd compiled. Foundations that might be convinced to help them bridge their funding gap if she could convince Uncle Emile to give her more time.

Lori folded herself over the porch rail and dangled her feet. "Where Duke?"

Ginny unlocked the main door and switched on the lights. "We won't be seeing him anymore."

"Why?"

The twinkling chandelier chased away the shadows, but a strange odor tainted the air. They'd have to open all the windows before the grand opening.

"Why?" Lori repeated, skipping inside.

"Because Duke's job here is finished and he'll be moving on."

"Why?"

"That's just how it is."

"Why?"

"It just is." Ginny let out a frustrated sigh and offered to show Lori her room while they waited for Uncle Emile.

Lori clomped up the stairs two at a time. "Duke loves me."

"Yes, he does." Ginny's voice hitched. Rick's affection for Lori couldn't have been an act. "But we can't always be with the people we love."

"Like Daddy?"

"Yes, like Daddy." Except Lori could be with *her* daddy, if only he wanted her.

While Lori explored her future room, Ginny watched for Uncle Emile's car.

"Look Gin!" Lori shouted from inside a cupboard.

Ginny glanced at her watch. Almost quarter to seven. Uncle Emile was usually so punctual. She walked over and peeked at the sliding shelves that had her sister so excited.

A car engine revved.

Ginny returned to the window, but couldn't spot Uncle Emile's car. "Come on, Lori. Let's go down and find Uncle Emile."

The door didn't budge.

Ginny jimmied the knob and tried again but the door still wouldn't open. "That's weird."

Lori bounced from one foot to the other, wagging her hands. "Let me out. See Emu."

"It's stuck." Ginny banged on the door. "Uncle Emile, we're up here. The door's stuck. Uncle Emile?"

Lori curled her hand into a fist and pounded the door, too. "Emu."

Ginny threw open a window. "Uncle Emile, are you out there?"

Someone darted from the shadow of the building toward the bush at the back of the property.

Rick's words slithered through her thoughts. *There are other ways.*

No, he wouldn't. Not after…

Not with her and Lori in the building.

This was it. Rick killed his truck lights and coasted to a stop outside Laud Developments. Darkness—cold and dank—crept in off the lake with the fog as he waited for the others to move into position.

Zach climbed into Rick's truck. "The warrant's on its way."

The mournful blast of a foghorn sounded in the distance. If not for the wan light slinking through the blinds of Laud's office, and the BMW parked outside, the place would look deserted.

"I knew this guy was cocky, but I didn't think he was stupid enough to stick around town after blowing away an undercover cop. What did he think? He could collect the insurance money and the community's sympathy, and the police wouldn't investigate him?" Rick plowed his fingers through his hair, flicking off crusts of blood.

Zach handed him a radio. "How do you want to do this?"

"You and your men fan the perimeter. I don't want him slipping away in the fog. I'm going through the front door."

"Are you sure you want to do that?"

"You better believe it. After everything I've sacrificed to nail this guy, I want to be the one to take him down."

The stench of rotting fish blew in from the rocky shoreline—a fitting backdrop for Rick's return from the dead.

A half-dozen uniformed officers joined them outside the truck. Rick walked a few paces to work out the stiffness in his injured knee.

Zach clipped out orders to his men then slapped a pair of handcuffs onto Rick's palm. "Remember, reasonable force."

Rick curled his fingers around the cold metal. "Yeah, I hear ya." With the way his head pounded, he didn't feel up to a fight, but he'd welcome an excuse to land one good punch. "Ready?"

On Zach's nod, Rick gave the signal and the officers disappeared around the building. Once outside the front doors, Rick radioed Zach. "Okay, we're going in." The officer at his side slammed the battering ram through the glass and Rick reached in to turn the latch. "I'm in."

Gun pointed to the floor, back to the wall, Rick edged toward Laud's office and kicked open the door. "Emile Laud, you're under arrest for—"

An empty room mocked him.

Police swarmed in. "Clear. Clear. Clear," sounded from every corner of the building.

Rick holstered his gun. Ginny smiled at him from a photo on the credenza. If he didn't nab Laud after all he'd put that woman through, he'd…

Rick swallowed the surge of anger and searched through the papers on Laud's desk for some clue to where he'd gone.

Zach strode in flanked by a uniformed officer. "I've issued a BOLO and got officers calling all the airports, train stations, bus stations and rental agencies within a fifty-mile radius."

"His yacht." Rick snapped open the blinds, but couldn't see through the thickening fog. A be-on-the-lookout alert wouldn't net many leads in this soup. "Send some men to the marina. His boat's the *Angelina*, dock thirty-two."

"Right." Zach jerked his head toward the door and the other officer rushed out. Zach's gaze zeroed in on the blinking red light of Laud's phone. He scrutinized the scrawls written beside the phone's extra buttons and punched one.

Ginny's voice—an urgent whisper punctuated by Lori's screeches—spewed from the speakerphone. "Where are you? I brought Lori up to see her room while we waited but—" The phone cut out.

Apparently, Rick's heart hadn't vacated his body, because Ginny's truncated message kicked it into a thunderous panic. He punched at buttons, desperate to hear the rest of the message. "What's she doing meeting Laud anywhere? When did that message come in? Why won't this play?"

Zach punched a number.

"Message sent, today, 6:42 p.m.," the computerized voice reported.

Zach punched another number and the message replayed.

"Can you tell what Lori's saying in the background?" Rick asked.

"Sounds like she's throwing a fit."

"Yeah, but listen." Rick hit the play button again.

"Emu, open door?" Zach gave Rick a bewildered look. "Doesn't make sense."

"She calls Emile Emu. What if he locked them in the building, too?"

"His own nieces?"

"You said yourself that once Laud figured out who I was there was no way he'd believe Ginny didn't know I was a cop."

"But Lori is his own daughter."

"A daughter he never wanted." Rick punched Ginny's number into the phone, his vision reddening. "Laud rigged the building to blow. He intended to kill us all."

"But if they were trapped at the group home you would've heard their screams."

A computer voice chirped. "The customer you are trying to reach is temporarily out of service."

Panic stormed Rick's chest.

Zach gripped his shoulders. "Listen to me. The

building isn't going to blow. You turned off the propane, dismantled the timer."

As Zach's words sank in, the vice around Rick's chest began to release.

"I'll send an officer over there to take a look. Okay?"

Brian skidded into the room. "We've got a GPS trace on Laud's cell phone. He's heading west on Highway Three toward Harbor Creek."

"I want to see a map." Rick snapped his fingers. "Now."

"It's on the computer screen in the reception area."

"Get these coordinates to our patrol cars." Rick shouldered past the crowd of officers studying the screen. "That's a lot of open fields. He could have a private plane stashed anywhere."

"No, the parachute club." Officer Tripp tapped her finger on the screen five miles ahead of Laud's location. "They offer private charter flights. I just got off the phone with a friend who works there. A plane's scheduled to take off in seven minutes, but the passenger—John Smith—hasn't arrived yet."

"Good work. Okay, I want you on the phone. No plane leaves that runway. Got it? I don't care what laws you have to threaten them with, just make sure they don't tip Laud off. Brian, I want you on this GPS." Rick grinned at Zach. "Looks like we have a plane to catch."

"I've got four patrol cars closing in on Laud's position." Zach loped toward his truck. "Do you want to ride with me?"

"No, we may need the extra vehicles to block him in. Keep your cell line open."

Since Zach had lights on the top of his truck, Rick followed behind him. He did a quick drumroll on the steering wheel. Finally, things were going his way. As he neared the road that led up to the group home, his pulse jumped. He beeped Zach. "Did you send an officer to the group home?"

"No, I'll do that now."

Gripped by an inexplicable urgency, Rick slammed his brakes. "Never mind. I'll go myself."

Zach's brake lights tapped on. "I can't wait around for you. If Laud takes off in that plane, we'll lose him for good. He'll be over the border and disappear along with any hope of justice for Tom."

Rick glanced at his watch. 6:58. Two minutes to take off. If Rick lost him now, his lies will have been for nothing.

But if he lost Ginny...

"I've gotta find Ginny. I can't shake the feeling she's in danger."

"Then maybe God's trying to tell you something. Her safety's more important than this collar. Some things really are black-and-white."

"Okay, I'm counting on you to get Laud." Rick pulled a U-turn. Ginny and Lori must've gotten to the group home after he left, which meant—Rick's breath froze in his chest—whoever locked them in could've set another timer.

Rick turned onto Carthill Drive and floored it. If he'd been honest with Ginny, she never would've trusted her uncle enough to step foot in that group home alone. His lies were going to get her killed.

He crested the hill. Was that a car coming down the group home driveway without its lights? A boxy, gray car?

Brake lights blipped on.

Rick swerved his truck in front of the approaching car and blocked the exit. As his headlights swept the car's interior, he glimpsed a female driver. Mary?

He jumped out of his truck and yanked open the door of her old Buick.

"Rick, what are you doing here?" Her distraught face paled under the glare of the car's interior light. Too distraught to realize her headlights weren't on?

"Have you been here this whole time?"

"He should have to suffer, like he's made me suffer," she said, her voice tinny, as though caught between the past and present.

"He'll suffer, Mary. Laud will go to jail for a long time." Rick talked as he would to a frightened child. "I'll take you home, okay? But first, I have to see if Ginny's still here. Have you seen her?"

"Ginny? No." Mary pulled the hood of her sweatshirt over her head. "What makes you think she'd be here?"

"She left a message at the office. Laud was supposed to meet her."

"You don't think he'd come back here after he left you for dead in the basement, do you?"

Rick glanced toward the building, dimly lit by exit

lights. Thanks to Mary, it stood unscathed. "I don't know, but I have to take a look."

"Wait." Mary grabbed his arm. "You can't go in. What if it's a setup? It's you he's after."

Rick hesitated. He'd underestimated the man once already. But even given Ginny's fury with him, Rick couldn't believe she'd make a crank call to lure him into another trap—at least, not knowingly. "I need to check it out."

"No!" Mary's nails dug into his arm, and the fear in her eyes clutched at his heart. She'd watched Tom die in a fire. Of course she'd fear the worst.

"I'll be careful. Wait here for me and then I'll see you home. All right?"

The putter of their engines filled the silence between them as he realized he'd have to pry her fingers from his arms.

A scream—Lori's?—sliced through the fog.

Rick tore Mary's hand loose and sprinted toward the building. "Call 9-1-1."

A faint glow shone from the rear of the second story. Lori's room.

Rick didn't dare call out and lose the chance to surprise their captor.

Muffled voices played off the churn of the distant surf. He pulled his gun, slipped through the front door and stole up the main staircase. Slowly, his eyes adjusted to the darkness.

Outside, gears screeched. An engine roared.

Mary must be moving his truck to open the driveway for the police. Good, it would distract Ginny's captor from his real threat—him. Because if the slime had hurt Ginny...

Thinking about what he wanted to do to the creep who'd been terrorizing her, Rick nearly ground his teeth to dust. With his back pressed to the wall, he peered around the corner and thanks to the light streaming from under the door at the end of the hall, could see that no one stood guard.

A hand slapped the door.

"Out!" Lori screamed.

"Shh," Ginny said. "Uncle Emile will be here soon."

Relief poured through Rick's body, slowing his racing heart. He holstered his gun and flipped on the hall light.

His heart stopped dead.

The door at the end of the hall was hockey-sticked—clamped closed by a clothes hanger wrapped around the doorknob. Who would do this? And what else had he done?

"Out," Lori wailed.

The sound wrenched Rick's heart into beating again. "Ginny, Lori, it's me, Rick. I'll get you out."

"Rick!" Lori clapped, but Ginny said nothing.

Rick checked for trip wires. Finding none, he untwisted the coat hanger, yanked out the hockey stick and shoved open the door.

Lori threw herself into his arms.

"It's okay, honey. You're okay. Let's get you outside."

"Emu, not come."

Over Lori's head, Rick met Ginny's glare—cold,

hateful, so utterly not Ginny—and he fought through the pain, grabbing his gut like he'd been drop-kicked. Of course, she thought he was behind this. A no-good, double-crossing liar who'd burn buildings for a price. "Ginny, I—"

She grabbed Lori's hand and pushed past him. "Save it for someone who'll believe you."

"Wait. I can explain."

The hall lights flickered out. Lori, already halfway down the stairs, screamed.

Rick sprinted after them. Hooking his arm around Lori's waist, he grabbed Ginny's hand. "Out, out, out!"

A sudden whoosh swept past them as if the building took a giant breath. And then—

"No-o-o!"

TWENTY-TWO

A fireball of heat and flames threw the trio to the gravelly dirt and Rick scrambled to cover Ginny and Lori's heads with his body. Falling debris glanced off his back.

Lori's fists bobbed in a frenetic rhythm. "Out," she uttered over and over, the sound muffled by throat-clogging tears.

Ginny struggled to her hands and knees. "How could you? This was Lori's home."

The accusation flayed Rick's chest, scraping his heart raw. "No. I didn't do this," he moaned. But he *had* failed her. In more ways than he'd imagined possible.

Blinking against the sting of smoke and regret, he prodded them forward, out of the reach of the ashes raining from the sky.

Ginny huddled next to Lori. Soot smeared their faces, except where tears trailed down their cheeks as they watched their dreams go up in smoke.

The wail of sirens drew closer.

Rick touched Ginny's hand. "I'm so sorry."

She wrapped her arms around Lori and edged away from him, as if she thought he might actually hurt them.

Why hadn't he listened to Zach and quit this case?

Because he loved her. He loved the way she protected her sister. Loved the way she gave so much of herself to make the special-needs kids feel truly special. Loved the way she'd made him feel special by letting him inside the hurting places in her heart.

Feeling utterly helpless, he stared at the flames eating everything he'd worked for, everything he'd wanted to give her.

Honks and sirens filled the air. Swirling lights stole through the haze. A fire truck barreled down the driveway, past his own lopsided vehicle—its lights still on—followed by another and another.

Before the pumper stopped, a firefighter jumped off the back, his arm hooked through the loops hanging from the attack line. A couple hundred feet of fabric hose spilled to the ground in a heap. Firefighters with axes and power saws directed ladders toward the roof. The first firefighter dragged his hose closer to the flames and braced himself, feet wide apart, hose curled into his stomach. Water charged along the line and the hose came alive, and the instant the water hit the flames, it flashed into steam.

Even this far from the blaze, the heat was claustrophobic.

Like that night at Tom's...wanting to run in after him, but repelled by the heat.

He should have to suffer, like he's made me suffer.

The recollection of Mary's tortured cry iced Rick's veins. He scanned the parking lot, the road. Mary's car was gone.

"No. Oh, please, God, no." Rick turned to Ginny. "When did Laud call you to meet him here?"

"He didn't. Mary did."

Rick's face went white—pasty white—like he might be sick, and a new fear rushed Ginny. "Where's my uncle?"

A loud crack split the air and the front of the group home crumbled in an explosion of black smoke and orange-blue flames.

Rick turned at the sound, his chest rising and falling in short bursts, his gaze fixed on the silhouette of men fighting a losing battle. "How could I have been so wrong?"

"What are you talking about? Where's Uncle Emile? If you hurt—" Ginny's insides seized at the wretched expression on Rick's face. She grabbed his arm. "What have you done?"

He groaned as if he hurt just to breathe, and for the first time she noticed the gash on his forehead, the blood matted in his hair. "Your uncle tried to kill me."

Ginny's heart jammed in her throat.

"And he killed Tom—the police officer who died in the townhouse fire." Rick spoke as if he had to tear out his insides to force out the words. "Your mom was right about him."

"No," Ginny screamed, tightening her hold on Lori. "I don't believe you. You're the one who suggested he burn…" Ginny bit at her fist, recalling her mom's words—appearances aren't always what they seem.

"Laud torches buildings for the money." Rick scrubbed his hand across his face. "I was trying to prove it."

"Over there," someone shouted, and pointed in their direction.

Two EMTs jogged across the uneven dirt toward them, tailed by a paunch-bellied guy in a sports jacket. "Are you three okay? Is anyone still in the building?"

Rick straightened. "It's all clear. I'm fine. Check them over."

The EMTs obeyed even though Rick was clearly in worse shape. Ginny pried Lori's arms from around her waist and coaxed her into letting the female EMT check her vitals.

As the other EMT, who could double as a linebacker, took Ginny's pulse, she strained to keep her eye on Rick. The way he took command of the situation the moment the EMTs arrived, like the way he'd taken charge when Mom took ill, as if it was second nature to him, was hard to ignore. His words—*I was trying to prove it*—replayed in her head. Was he working for the police? An informant?

Rick shook hands with the guy in the sports jacket.
"Who's he?" Ginny asked the EMT.

"Cop. Drake I think he said his name was."

"How'd you get here so fast?" Rick asked the question like he knew the cop, expected him even.

"Anonymous tip—bomb threat."

Ginny gasped. Someone despised the group home enough to blow it up?

But that meant the explosion had nothing to do with Rick, or Uncle Emile. So Rick hadn't tried to kill her and Lori. He'd come to save them. But how did he know?

"The tipster female?" Rick's question sounded more like a groan.

"Yeah." The officer quirked his head. "How'd you know?" He glanced Ginny's way and she jerked back behind the screen of her linebacker EMT.

Rick's shoulders sagged as if the energy had drained out of him. "You need to send a car to pick up Mary, but go easy on her."

"Tom's wife? What's she got to do with this?"

"She was here. Agitated." Rick's gaze drifted to the flames and the sadness Ginny glimpsed tugged at something deep inside her. "Mary said she wanted Laud to suffer like she'd suffered."

Ginny's pulse jumped. Mary was Tom's wife? As in the cop, Tom, who died in the townhouse fire?

"She's not well," Rick continued. "I think she targeted Laud's nieces to hurt him. Perhaps in her mind, the loss of his loved ones by arson would be the sweetest irony." Rick pressed his fingers to his eyes. "I'm just glad I got here in time to save them."

Shivers seized Ginny's body. The kind of shivers that clattered her teeth and rattled her limbs as if she'd just been plucked from icy water instead of a blazing inferno. The sensation swirled through her chest, sending her heart into juddering spasms.

Rick talked as if he loved her. Loved her despite her accusations.

She pushed away the EMT's stethoscope and stepped toward Rick.

The officer clapped him on the back. "You did a good job. Zach called in a few minutes ago. Laud's pilot refused to take off in the fog. Laud was sitting on the plane on the runway when our men arrived."

Our? Our! As in Rick included? "You're a cop?"

He didn't answer, and she didn't know what to make of his pained expression.

The officer squeezed Rick's shoulder. "One of my best. His instincts saved your life."

Ginny stared at the officer as if he was speaking Swahili, even as Kim's pronouncement—he'd make an amazing cop; he's got great instincts—boomed in her head.

He's a cop. A cop!

Images tumbled through her mind. The way he took down Robins at church, Eddie at the gala. The way he interrogated her about her brakes and Mom about Uncle Emile. The way he intimated Uncle Emile could do something about his money problems. How could she have been so blind?

But if he was a cop, that meant…

He wasn't an ex–gang member. He wasn't an arsonist. He wasn't…in Miller's Bay to make a fresh start.

"Why didn't you tell me you were a cop?" she shrilled.

The officer stepped back. "I'll give you a few minutes. But, Rick, we'll need statements before these ladies go home."

Rick, his eyes glued to hers, gave his *real* boss a brisk nod.

Lori clung to Ginny's middle. "Want go home."

"We can't yet."

Rick gave Lori a sympathetic smile. "I can take you home. I'll let Drake know that I'll bring your statement in later."

Behind him dark figures in turnout gear, now barely visible except for the gleam of headlights on reflective strips, snuffed out the last of the flames, while policemen unraveled caution tape, setting a perimeter around the surreal scene.

Suddenly overwhelmed by how close they'd come to dying, Ginny gave a silent nod.

Rick's fingers grazed the small of her back as they walked toward his truck, but she resisted the urge to lean into him.

The sway of the truck lulled Lori into slumber, and they drove in silence until Ginny couldn't stand it a second longer. "Why didn't you tell me you were a cop?"

"When we met I was working undercover on the

fringes of a gang." He glanced at her, apology in his eyes. "I couldn't risk a leak."

"A leak? You couldn't possibly have thought I'd tell on you."

"No, I never thought that. The deception was for your protection. Not mine."

She pictured the anguish in his eyes when she'd left him standing outside the restaurant fifteen months ago. Yes, he'd thought he was protecting her. He was exactly the honorable guy she'd first believed, and she felt horrible for ever doubting him.

All these years she'd been so critical of people who misjudged Lori because of appearances, and here she'd done the same thing. Worse than that, she'd let herself be duped by Uncle Emile's polished performance.

"But you could've explained once you finished the case," Ginny said. "How could you let me keep believing you were a criminal?"

He pulled into her driveway, shifted into park and stared straight ahead.

Understanding flared. "You were counting on it. You *wanted* me to tell my uncle. Didn't you? Our relationship was just one big ruse."

"Let's get your sister inside."

Ginny scrambled out of the truck. What had she expected him to do? Argue?

Yes, and more than that, deny that he'd used her to get closer to her uncle.

Rick lifted Lori into his arms and carried her to her room. When he laid her on the bed as if she were a precious baby, Ginny bit back a rush of raw emotions. How could she have fallen so completely in love with someone who'd done nothing but lie to her?

After he left the room, Ginny slid off Lori's shoes, tucked the blanket around her and then found Rick in the living room. He stood by the picture window, and their eyes met in the reflection.

"Tell me the truth. You came to Miller's Bay to arrest my uncle and you used me to get to him, didn't you?"

Rick breathed a pained *yes*.

Ginny sank into a chair. "I was wrong. The truth hurts more than the lie."

"I never lied about my feelings for you." Rick dropped to one knee in front of her. "I never wanted to hurt you. Please believe me. I hated keeping the truth from you."

She steeled herself against the desperation in his voice. "If you really cared about me, you would've told me the truth as soon as you finished the gang job."

"No, *because* I cared about you, I stayed away. My job is dangerous, and that danger could spill over into the lives of those I care about." He clutched her hands. "I didn't want that for you."

The tenderness of his words made her want to believe him, to believe *in* him, the way she should have all along. She may not have known his name or his job, but she'd known his character. That hadn't changed.

"So you stayed away. What about now?" She

stroked his cheek, wishing she could erase the reminders of danger the day had scrawled across his face. The bruise on his forehead, the soot smeared under his eyes, the smell of smoke in his clothes. "Because in case you haven't noticed, your strategy didn't spare me from anything. Except maybe a chance to know the real Rick Gray."

"It's just that—" His gaze dropped to their clasped hands. "If something happened to you because of my job, I could never live with myself."

Ginny gently turned his face back toward hers. "But tonight you chose me over your job."

He touched the bruise on his forehead and gave her a lopsided smile. "Almost dying helped me straighten out my priorities. Ginny…"

His lips brushed across hers and every cell of her body came alive.

"You're more important to me than any arrest. I love you so much. I don't want to stay away anymore."

Her heart felt as if it might burst. She walked her fingers teasingly along his chest. "Hmm, I don't know what to say. First you're a gang member, then an arsonist, now you're a cop. Will it always be this way?"

He closed his hand over hers, but the smile in his eyes blinked out. "I'm an undercover cop. There will be times when I can't tell you where I am or what I'm doing."

Memories surfaced of Mom's lonely vigils when Dad was out of contact on one secret mission or another. Mom and Dad smiled at Ginny from their wedding picture on the mantel. Dad in his uniform, Mom in a white gown—believing in happily ever afters.

But real life seldom played out like the fairy tales.

And if Ginny was honest with herself, she'd have to admit that deep inside she feared she couldn't cope with Rick's dual life…or the fact he had a dangerous job like her dad had.

She slipped her hand from beneath his, clenching it against the ache in her chest. "I'm sorry. I can't live like that."

TWENTY-THREE

Rick stood at the end of his driveway and lobbed the basketball in a perfect arc. He could almost hear the swish, then like everything else he'd done lately, the ball hit the rim and bounced back to catch him in the gut. He dribbled—no, pounded the ball—up the pavement and slammed it into the basket.

Basketball usually helped work off the stress after a hard case, but two weeks of slamming baskets hadn't worked Ginny out of his system. He caught the rebound and hunched over to haul in a breath. He couldn't think straight for missing her. The pain in his chest hurt so bad, last night he'd torn off his shirt and stared in the mirror, certain he'd find a gaping hole where his heart used to be.

Something in the town's water must've messed up his brain, because he'd completely deluded himself into thinking that once he told Ginny he was a cop, she'd see past his deceit to the man underneath. He flung the ball at the garage door. "Why am I hanging on to a job that stands in the way of the woman I love?"

"Good question."

Rick spun around to find Zach leaning against his pickup, legs outstretched, arms crossed over his chest. "When did you get here?"

Zach nudged up his ball cap with his thumb. "Some time between the bent basketball rim and the dented garage door. You want to talk about it?"

"No."

"Funny…" Zach scooped up the ball and swished it into the basket. "Ginny said the same thing."

Eagerness for details sprang up in Rick, like a dog begging for scraps, but he pitched his voice as if news about Ginny didn't interest him in the least. "Oh, yeah?"

From the look of Zach's smirk, he wasn't buying the indifference routine. "Let's just say Kim and I have compared notes." Zach lined up another shot. "I visited Mary this morning."

Rick caught the ball and absorbed another jab of failure. The night of the fire he'd thought his revelation about Laud had prompted her to lure Ginny and Lori to the group home to avenge her husband's death, but she'd known about Laud all along, had been plotting her revenge for weeks. Rick should've recognized the signs of a woman on the edge. And her boxy gray car. And the way she ran in a hooded sweatshirt. Some detective he'd turned out to be. "How'd she know Laud was behind the fire that killed Tom?"

"She didn't, for sure. Not until you started working for him. She confessed to everything—trashing your house so you wouldn't know she'd searched it, sabotaging Ginny's brakes, hurling the rock and tossing the two-by-four from the window, snitching to the labor board, luring Ginny and Lori to the group home."

"So she snatched the photo of Tom and me. I should've known."

"You never should've been on the case. You weren't thinking straight. She's sorry for hurting you. If she'd realized you loved Ginny, I don't think she would've tried to hurt her."

"Great. Pile on a little more guilt, why don't you?"

"What's eating you? You kept Ginny safe. You got your man. Mary will get the help she needs. What more do you want?"

"Uh, a home for Ginny's sister." Rick flung the ball at the net, caught the rebound and flung it again. *When this case is over, we're over.* He'd known it. Didn't mean he had to like it. And if Zach planned to toss the words back in his face, he could leave. Now.

Zach intercepted the ball and, daring Rick to reclaim it, dribbled down the driveway. "Why don't you just tell the woman you love her?"

"I did."

Zach must've heard the pain in Rick's voice, because he stopped dribbling and stared. "What did she say?"

"That she can't live with a cop."

"She said that?"

Rick slapped the ball away. "More or less." He took a shot. Missed.

"So quit."

"I can't. If I hadn't strong-armed the captain into letting me pursue Laud, he'd still be walking around, preying on innocent victims."

Zach grabbed Rick's arm and jerked him to a halt. "You have a choice."

"No." Rick yanked his arm free. "I don't."

"Two months ago, I might've believed that. Clearly, your crusade was more important to you than being honest with the only woman you've ever loved."

"Crusade? Is that what you think this was?"

"You're sacrificing a future with Ginny so you can hunt down bad guys for the rest of your life. What would you call it?"

Rick thrust the ball into Zach's chest and stalked toward the house. "I don't want to talk about it."

"The night you risked losing Laud to make sure Ginny was safe, I thought you'd finally figured it out."

"What?" Rick spun around. "What did I figure out?"

"You don't have to carry the entire game. You trusted me to stop Laud and I did."

"What's that got to do with Ginny?"

"You chose her over your case. So you see, you've already made the right choice. You're just having a hard time getting around to accepting it."

"I made my dad a promise. I can't quit."

"You're not alone."

Rick ground his teeth until his jaw ached. He'd never felt more alone in his entire life. But Zach didn't need to know it.

"Look, man, I don't want you to quit. I know you made a promise to your dad. And you're a good cop. But you've forgotten God's on your side. Did Drake tell you what time that bomb was supposed to go off?"

"No."

"Laud hired Jones to set it for seven. That's why Mary lured Ginny and Lori there. But Jones chickened out when he saw Ginny go into the building, and Mary had to set it herself."

Seven o'clock? It had been all of that when he confronted her in the driveway. There was no way he could've gotten to Ginny and Lori in time.

"God had your back. He doesn't need you. But He wants to use you. Problem is you're so busy trusting in your own strength, your own plans, you haven't considered that maybe God has different plans."

"Okay, I'll admit I've been slacking off where God's concerned. But my life is in His hands every second I'm out there. I know that."

"Yeah, but are you willing to play it His way? There's a lot more to you than just being a cop. Maybe it's time to let go…and let God."

"Now you're quoting me bumper stickers?"

"You'd prefer Bible verses?"

Rick stole the ball and dribbled down the driveway.

"Nothing's going to bring your parents back, you know?"

Rick fumbled his layup and smashed shoulder-first into the garage door. "What?"

"Nailing Laud hasn't filled the hole in your chest any more than hurting Ginny and Lori would've taken away Mary's pain. Only God can do that."

"That's *not* why I'm a cop. God's called me to serve the cause of justice." He thumped his fist against his chest. "I know it in here."

"There are other ways to serve justice. You're great working with the youth at the community center. If you kept those kids off the street and gave them hope in a future free of crime, it would go a long way to cleaning up this county."

"Volunteering at the community center won't pay the bills."

Utter disbelief twisted Zach's expression. "You know what? You don't deserve Ginny."

"Don't you think I know that?"

"Is that what this is really about? You don't think you deserve her, so you hide behind your promise to your dad, and tell yourself that letting her go is somehow noble?"

"She's a black-and-white kind of person. And I live in shades of gray."

"But never in here." Zach poked Rick's chest. "There's no room for shades of gray in your heart. A good cop has to believe in what he does, and you do. Your partners know they can count on you no matter what. That's truth. That's what Ginny needs to hear."

"Yeah? Well, it wasn't enough."

"You're a real piece of work. You know that?

She didn't brush you off because you're a cop. She brushed you off because you can't even be honest with yourself."

Rick turned his back and stalked toward the house. The basketball flew past his head and slammed into the garage door with a crash.

"Listen to me, because I'm only going to say this once. A love like Ginny's comes around once in a lifetime, and you'd better cling to it with everything you've got, because one day you're going to wake up and realize God wanted to give you so much more than you were willing to let Him. And you threw it away."

"It's easy to dispense advice when it's somebody else's life on the line," Rick snapped. "Have you ever even had a serious relationship?"

Zach sucked in a breath as if he'd been punched in the gut. As if maybe he knew what he was talking about…from experience. His mouth opened, then shut, then he stormed down the driveway. "Forget it. If you want to throw your life away, you go right ahead. I won't stop you." He climbed into his truck and roared away.

Terrific. He'd lost his girl. Now his best friend had bailed on him, too. Rick hurled the ball at the net and missed completely. "I guess it's just You and me, God."

The wind rustled the leaves, as if God might be trying to get his attention.

"I know I need to apologize, but Zach doesn't

understand. What I do is not a crusade. I'm not
trying to bring my dad back. I've wanted to be a
cop since I was ten years old." He hadn't lied about
that to Ginny.

There's a lot more to you than just being a cop.

"Lord, I'm not seeing it the way Zach sees it, but
he was right about one thing. I have been going it
alone and trusting in my own strength. I'm sorry
about that."

Spurred by a compulsion to recover the dove he'd
given Ginny, Rick grabbed his truck keys and drove
to the police station. By the time he arrived, the im-
poundment lot was deserted.

Rick reached through the shattered windshield of
the blistered car and lifted the ornament from the
sooty water pooled on the dash. He'd clean it up and
return it to Ginny—a reminder of God's protection
where he'd failed.

Rick tapped bits of glass from the surface. Like
the dove's, he'd watched Ginny's world crash around
her. He'd probably never be able to erase from his
memory the stark fear he'd seen in her eyes when he
freed her from the locked room, or the horror he'd
heard in her voice. How had he let things get so far
off course that she'd actually believed he could torch
her sister's home?

*She didn't brush you off because you're a cop. She
brushed you off because you can't even be honest
with yourself.*

"Oh, God, I love her." Rick swallowed hard,

crushed the dove to his chest. "I can hardly breathe when I try to imagine life without her."

Ginny's sweet voice whispered through his thoughts. *You chose me.*

Rick dropped to his knees on the chewed-up pavement. "I did, Lord. I do. Whatever it takes. Because as much as I love being a cop, if Ginny doesn't want me to be one, I'll quit." He looked skyward. "If that's okay with You. Please, show me what to do. I don't want to wake up one day and realize I've thrown away the sweetest gift You've ever given me."

Ginny handed the last player a bib, then pulled out a bat and ball.

Kim stalked toward her. "Now you've gone and done it. Rick quit."

"Of course he quit. You could hardly expect him to come back and help coach T-ball after I…" Ginny struggled for a nice way to describe what she'd done.

Kim propped her hands on her hips. "Broke his heart?"

"Yeah, that."

"I thought you would've come to your senses by now."

"I have. I'm moving on. The fundraising money was recovered, and I'm working with Mr. Castleman's foundation to raise the rest of what we'll need to rebuild the group home."

"Have you told Rick?"

Ginny handed the bat and ball to the parent who'd

volunteered to be today's batting coach. "I told you, Rick and I aren't seeing each other anymore."

"But he loves you."

"I'm not sure either of us knows what love is. The first test of my faith in him, I failed. If I truly loved him, how could I have believed he was capable of arson?"

"Because he told you."

Ginny jerked up her arms. "Exactly."

"No, you don't get it. You trusted him so much that you couldn't believe he'd lie to you. That's why you believed what he said."

"What does it matter? How can I love someone when I can't even tell if they're speaking the truth?"

"The same way you love these kids, by seeing them through God's eyes. You see the heart inside that's trying so hard to be good and true. Despite Rick's lies, you saw that in him, too. You knew in your heart his motives were pure."

Ginny crossed her arms over the festering ache in her chest. "I told him I couldn't live that way and he didn't even try to talk me out of it." *Oh Lord, is that what I'd been hoping? That he wouldn't give up on us so easily? Would I have been willing to risk my heart if he'd asked?*

"Seems to me he was showing his love. By not being self-seeking."

Ginny returned her attention to the game. "Whatever. It doesn't change how I feel."

"You know what? You're right. You say lies hurt more than the truth. And you're living proof. You've been moping around, lying to yourself. Trying to convince yourself you don't love him and he doesn't love you. When the truth is, he loves you so much, he quit the police force."

"What?" She grabbed Kim's arm. "When? How do you know?"

"Zach called me."

"I thought the two of you weren't dating anymore."

"That doesn't mean we've stopped talking. He told me that his boss tried to convince Rick to take a vacation to reconsider, but Rick held his ground."

Rick's voice flooded Ginny's thoughts. *My hero was an off-duty police officer. I decided then and there I wanted to be just like that man when I grew up.* All those weeks, she'd longed for Rick to open up to her…and he already had. He'd shared his dream, his life, and she'd shot it down. She shot him down. The one man who'd peered past the external and loved the person hiding inside. She'd loved him for that more than anything and yet she'd failed to truly return his love. "He can't do this."

"Why? You're supposed to be happy. He's got to be doing it for you."

"But I can't let him, don't you see?"

"No, you're not making any sense. You told him you couldn't live with a cop. So-o-o, he's choosing you! I'm picturing music, flowers, shouts of glee…." Kim leaned close and lowered her voice. "I do's."

"No. I fell in love with Rick Gray—the cop. I might not have known he was a cop, but— Oh, don't you see? If I let him do this, it's as though I can't accept and love him for who he is."

"Uh! News flash—you don't. The fact he's a cop gives you the heebie-jeebies."

"But his willingness to quit proves how wrong I was. He's wanted to be a cop all his life. He's good at it. You said yourself, he's got great instincts."

Kim's eyes gleamed and her smile spread from ear to ear.

"Those instincts saved my life." Ginny shook Kim's arm to snag her wandering attention. "I've got to find him."

"I'm right here." Rick's rumbly voice trembled down Ginny's spine. When her gaze found his, the love written in his clear blue eyes swept her breath away. He trailed his finger along her cheek, igniting every nerve ending. "You wanted to see me?"

Her racing pulse practically hurled her into his arms. She placed her hand on his chest to stop herself. Beneath her palm his heart mimicked her own runaway thudding.

He covered her hand with his—warm and tender—and took a step closer. His breath whispered across her cheek as his eyes roamed her face, finally settling on her lips.

She swallowed, but her heart remained firmly jammed in her throat. "Rick, I can't let you do this."

His hand tightened around hers and the emotion in his eyes turned achingly raw.

"I mean, you can't quit."

"Too late. It's done."

"But—"

He stopped her words with a touch. "No buts. I choose you."

His tender voice confirmed the truth God had been growing in her heart. "But, I don't want you to quit."

He tilted his head with an adorable look of confusion.

"I fell in love with a man who loves justice and serves it well, and if that's where God's calling you to be, I need to trust He'll carry us through the hard times."

"Us." He cradled her face in his hands. The gleam in his eye turned her legs to jelly. "I like the sound of that." He kissed her, sweetly, as if holding back, keenly aware of all the young eyes watching from the ball diamond. Her honorable hero.

When he pulled away, she felt a blush spread across her face at the simmering promise in his eyes of many more kisses to come.

The T-ball team burst into thunderous applause and Lori hurtled into Rick's arms. "Duke back!"

Rick lifted her off the ground and twirled her in a big circle. "Yes, I'm back to stay!"

EPILOGUE

Rick scooped Ginny into his arms and carried her toward the newly constructed house—a blue-sided bungalow with a wide front porch—just like the dream home she'd described. All that was missing was the white picket fence and a swing set.

She cuddled against him. "What are you doing?"

"I'm carrying you over the threshold."

Her eyes went round and her soft pink lips formed a perfect *O* to match.

He dipped his head and kissed those lips, exploring their sweetness before he set her down in the front hall of her new home. "Ta-da-a!"

"Rick?" Her smile quivered. "Whose house is this?"

"Ours." He slipped his hands around her waist and drew her into the circle of his arms. "If you'll have me. Do you like it? I built a separate apartment on the side for your Mom and Lori."

Ginny flung her arms around his neck. "I can't believe you kept this a secret."

"Do you forgive me?" He feathered kisses along

her jaw and the sweet sound of her laughter wound its way around his heart. He held out a small box. When she looked inside, he couldn't help but grin as her smile dropped a fraction.

"My dove! You rescued her." Ginny hugged his neck. "I'll hang it in my new car."

"Uh, you may want to remove her necklace first."

Ginny looked at the ornament again, and this time spotted the diamond ring threaded around her neck. "Oh!"

Slipping off the ring, Rick dropped to one knee and took Ginny's hand in his. "This ring is to remind you that your love means more to me than any job. Although I've agreed to go back to being a cop— never undercover—I need you to know that I love you best and first. The truth I will always give you is I love you." He slid the ring onto her finger, then lifted her fingers to his lips. "Will you marry me?"

"Yes, yes, yes."

She launched herself into his arms, and his heart filled with happiness, knowing that after days of walking shadows to do his job, he could always come home to the light of love in Ginny's eyes.

* * * * *

Dear Reader,

I'm thrilled that you chose to spend a few hours reading my novel. Thank you.

Between my research for this series and struggling alongside my hero as he wrestled with the need to lie to protect his cover, my respect for law enforcement officers has heightened immeasurably. I can't wait to share more of their stories in this Undercover Cop series.

I love reading romantic suspense, especially inspirationals, because watching characters work through problems often gives me fresh insights into Scripture, and empathy for others in similar circumstances. I hope this story has similarly inspired you.

Thank you again for reading DEEP COVER. I'd love to hear your thoughts. Contact me at SandraOrchard@ymail.com or c/o Harlequin Books, Love Inspired Suspense, 233 Broadway, Suite 1001, New York, NY 10279. To learn about my next Love Inspired Suspense, visit me online at www.SandraOrchard.com. Look for Kim's story, *Shades of Truth,* in March 2012.

Wishing you abundant blessings,
Sandra Orchard

Questions for Discussion

1. Rick Gray desperately wants Ginny to see him as honorable. What does it mean to you to be honorable? Do you believe Rick is honorable? Is there a difference between trying to appear honorable and being honorable?

2. Which character in the story do you most easily relate to and why?

3. Rick struggles with lying to Ginny in order to protect his cover. Yet, he doesn't question lying to bring criminals to justice. He holds to the maxim that the end justifies the means, even if those means are contrary to God's Word. Do you agree? Why or why not?

4. Ginny is quick to assume the worst about both her mom and Rick because of their past mistakes. Yet, she trusts her uncle, the true bad guy, implicitly. How do past experiences hinder you from seeing people for who they really are? How might you look past their actions to the hurting person inside?

5. At the end of the story, Rick realizes that he's been trusting in his own strength to protect Ginny, rather than God's. Believers often seek

God's help or guidance as a last resort. Do you? Why or why not?

6. Rick observes that Ginny accepts the mentally challenged children she works with for who they are and thereby helps them believe that God does, too. What actions can you take to demonstrate to those around you that God loves them where they're at?

7. Rick tells Ginny that most people think they have to clean up their lives before God will forgive them, accept them, love them, and that although she *knows* that's hogwash, her heart denies her the experience of His grace. Is there something in your life that's separating you from God? How can you change that situation?

8. Ginny says to Rick, "I've taken care of Mom and Lori my whole life. When they're gone, I'll have no one. Be no one." Does your sense of worth and identity come from what you do or who you're with? Where does God want it to come from?

9. Emile Laud is driven by ambition. He wants people to believe he's wealthy and altruistic so they'll admire him, because as a child he was scoffed at for being poor and unpopular. What are the consequences of his obsession? Do you un-

consciously try to fill a deep-rooted need in ways that might lead to unwelcome consequences?

10. Rick gave Ginny a dove ornament as a reminder that God watches over her. Do you have a symbol or verse or song or keepsake that reminds you of God's love when He feels far away? If not, do you think having such a reminder on display would help to center your thoughts on God?

11. Ginny envies her sister's childlike faith. She says, "I wish I could be like Lori and run to Rick with arms opened wide, freely forgiving, trusting that he's changed." Is there something hindering you from forgiving someone who's hurt you? What can you do to remedy the situation?

12. Ginny says, "I'd rather know the truth than be lied to out of some misguided notion that I'll somehow be happier or safer." Yet, we often sugarcoat the truth to spare others' feelings. (For example, every smart husband knows how not to answer the question "Honey, does this dress make me look fat?") Can you remember a time when you've sugarcoated the truth? Did your words help or hinder the other person's understanding of themselves or their circumstances? Would you do it again? Why or why not?

LARGER-PRINT BOOKS!

**GET 2 FREE
LARGER-PRINT NOVELS
PLUS 2 FREE
MYSTERY GIFTS**

Love Inspired

SUSPENSE
RIVETING INSPIRATIONAL ROMANCE

Larger-print novels are now available...

LARGER-PRINT BOOKS!

**GET 2 FREE
LARGER-PRINT NOVELS
PLUS 2 FREE
MYSTERY GIFTS**

Larger-print novels are now available...

INSPIRATIONAL

Inspirational romances to warm your heart & soul.

SUSPENSE

LARGER PRINT

TITLES AVAILABLE NEXT MONTH

Available October 11, 2011

NIGHTWATCH
The Defenders
Valerie Hansen

THE CAPTAIN'S MISSION
Military Investigations
Debby Giusti

PRINCESS IN PERIL
Reclaiming the Crown
Rachelle McCalla

FREEZING POINT
Elizabeth Goddard

ISBN-13:978-0-373-67480-0

IDENTITY: GUARDED

Maintaining his cover cost undercover cop Rick Gray the woman he loved. Sweet Ginny Bryson never really knew Rick—he never gave her the chance. Not then, and not now, when he's back with a new alias to gather evidence against Ginny's uncle. The man's crimes led to Rick's partner's death, and Rick wants justice to be served. But his investigation is stirring up trouble, and Ginny is smack-dab in the middle. Someone wants *Ginny* to pay the price for what her uncle has done. But how can Rick protect her without blowing his cover, jeopardizing his assignment...and risking both their lives?

Undercover Cops:
Fighting for justice puts their lives—and hearts—on the line.

$6.50 U.S./$7.50 CAN.

ISBN-13:978-0-373-67480-0

50650

9 780373 674800

a LOVE INSPIRED®
SUSPENSE book from

HARLEQUIN

www.Harlequin.com